STEVEN LEA

Out Of The Equation

For my wife, just because...

Acknowledgement

Thank you to all the people who read and review my books.
You make my day.

I

Nassau, Bahamas

Prologue

Only Dave Martin heard the faint thunk on the hull of the fishing boat when the body hit it. Everyone else was laughing, drinking or snoring, or a combination of all three. He'd begun to regret inviting his college buddies onto his boat for the weekend for a trip from Fort Lauderdale to Bimini, but he'd foolishly wanted to show off. Isn't that what having your own boat is about? Showing your friends you're doing OK. He'd never really even been a big fisherman, but he knew a couple of his friends were and they'd appreciate the chance to take a trip, just like old times. They were all in their late thirties and married now, most had kids, so party weekends like this were few and far between now. It was a rarity they all jumped at when he offered.

The trip over to Bimini, roughly halfway between Fort Lauderdale and Nassau, had been idyllic, bouncing over the waves in blazing early morning sunshine, landing in Bimini, and drinking on the beach before heading out looking for fish. They'd had some luck but came back early to drink some more and had a late night, so today Bradley suggested they go out later and fish in the dark, maybe go out further and deeper, looking for tuna or sailfish. Charlie caught a big one early on so the others lost hope and the drinking started again. Tom had fallen asleep an hour ago – such a lightweight, same as in university.

Michael was smoking outside at the stern of the twenty-five-foot boat when, in a two-second lull in the conversation Dave heard the thunk of something solid against the hull. He looked around thinking someone had dropped a bottle or glass on the floor. Tom was snoring on the bench, Charlie was sitting on the floor, trying to tell an old story about their college days that nobody remembered. Bradley was keeping an eye on the wheel. Dave almost dismissed the noise but through the fog of three or four beers, he stood up to go and investigate.

Stumbling across the floor in the cramped cabin they were sheltering in from the short, sharp shower they'd had an hour or so ago, he opened the door and stepped outside onto the deck near the bow on the port side, adjusting his legs to balance and breathing in a deep gulp of Atlantic evening air. In the dark he could see very little and had handed over navigation to Bradley earlier, who was a keen sailor and therefore least inebriated. Just as Dave turned around to head back inside he leaned out to scan the hull where he thought he'd heard the noise come from. In the inky black water there was a patch of white that looked like a large cloth, which could've fallen off the edge of the boat earlier in the evening.

Dave squinted his eyes and re-focussed and decided there was a collar on the cloth which, he calculated in his haze, must mean it was a shirt. A couple of seconds later the realization of what that meant began to dawn. His heart began to beat faster and the alcohol-induced fog began to clear. Dave looked either side of the shirt and saw hands, feet and a face. Standing up straight and swinging his head from side to side to look for a pole, he shouted, "Help!" instinctively before stumbling back towards the cabin and flinging the door wide open. Bradley

4

heard his cry, Michael was making his way round from the back of the boat, Charlie looked annoyed that no-one was listening to him, and Tom was still asleep.

"There's a body," said Dave as he pointed behind him and promptly threw up. Bradley grabbed Dave and sat him down before going out through the door and grabbing a net on a long pole to start to reach for the body where Dave had pointed. Michael joined him and helped him land their biggest catch of the day.

"We need help!" shouted Bradley.

Charlie wandered out and joined in the effort. Dave worried the boat might tip if they all went over that side and sat next to sleeping Tom, confident his friends would manage without him. He started clearing some space for the new arrival and shook Tom by the shoulder to wake him up and make some room.

Michael, Charlie and Bradley dragged the sopping wet body into the cabin and slumped on the floor beside it and stared at each other.

"Get on the radio," said Michael, pointing at the large cluster of lights on the ship gracefully sailing away behind them into the darkness. "He's probably fallen off that."

Chapter 2

Killing the boss of a drug cartel is a big deal. A very big deal. Killing him accidentally is foolish, to say the least. There's a long list of consequences to go through in your head before you decide your next move. But Maria Cortez was distracted and had no time to worry about that yet. She was distracted at first by the noise as the front of her rented Corolla slammed into the back of a Jaguar saloon owned by Ernesto Gutierrez, the aforementioned cartel boss, crushing the front of her car and the rear of his into a barely recognisable mess. She'd never crashed a car before, least of all deliberately, so hadn't expected this much damage when she'd floored the pedal fifty metres away and deliberately driven into his car in an attempt to stop the gunfight that looked likely to break out. She was also distracted by the bodies that jumped or were knocked out of the way, that had been standing at the side or in front of the car, which she'd been too focussed to notice when she'd made her decision. Only then, when the dust started to settle, did she become distracted by the thought of what might happen as a consequence of what she'd just done.

About twenty meters in front of the Jaguar, on the other side of the road and facing towards the wreckage was a large black SUV also owned by Ernesto Gutierrez, and usually driven by one or other of his security men. Standing behind its open hatchback, having earlier stolen the SUV from Gutierrez in an attempt to escape from his clutches, John Barker was holding an automatic rifle he'd pulled out of the boot just seconds before when the stand-off between them had reached its peak. Gutierrez had followed the SUV's tracker to the storage unit where Barker had hidden a dozen holdalls containing the (almost) twenty million in cash that Maria had stolen from her ex-husband Michael on board the cruise ship Starlight a week or so before. Barker had managed to divert the bank transfer into his account as it happened, and then drawn it out from a local bank over the course of a week and hidden it there.

The sight of this anonymous-looking, averagely-built Englishman holding that sort of weapon was incongruous. Even though he'd been a policeman in London for a number of years, he wasn't used to this. He looked like he needed some help.

"Open the glove box," Maria said to Stephen Mitchell, sitting beside her in the passenger seat, who was just getting the air back into his lungs after the impact he'd known was coming but had still taken the wind out of his sails.

"What?" Stephen said, wondering what could be in there that would be useful right now.

"Open the glovebox! Quickly! There's a gun in there," Maria said, answering his question.

Stephen did as he was told and, after a split-second's hesitation as he debated internally whether it was a good idea to give a weapon to this woman he'd only met barely twenty-four hours ago, decided she was probably on his side for now, and handed it over. Maria grabbed it and immediately opened her door and jumped out. Stephen felt he should do the same, but as soon as he did he remembered he had no weapon himself, so squatted down behind the open door, hoping it would give him some protection if anyone started shooting.

As Maria stood up and raised both arms to hold the gun in front of her, she saw in her peripheral vision two people running away: a man to her left, and a woman on the right hand side of the car. Jose Ramirez, the chief engineer of the Starlight cruise ship, and his opposite number from the admin department, Mary Tkachuk. Either of them could easily have tackled her to the ground at that point if they'd wanted to but that clearly wasn't on their agenda. They had stepped out of the rear of the car seconds before the impact and had escaped uninjured. But why run? Maria was about to find out.

Directly in front of her, Carlo, Gutierrez's bodyguard, was picking himself up off the road where he'd been hit in the back by the rear door of the Jaguar when it shunted forward a couple of meters. He fumbled around for the gun he'd been about to aim at Barker and stood up, only to hear someone shout, "Don't, Carlo! Don't even think about it."

Carlo recognised Maria's voice without turning round because she had been living with Ernesto until a few days ago when he'd discovered her secret attempts to find the cash that he was chasing Barker down for, believing it to be rightfully his. Ernesto had instructed his security team to dispose of her and Carlo had assumed there was no chance of her turning up again. Clearly someone hadn't done their job properly, or Maria was more of a force to be reckoned with than even he had thought.

Carlo straightened up and stiffened his body, but only half-turned his head, trying to keep both Barker in front and to the right of him, and now Maria partly behind him, in his peripheral vision.

"Whose side are you on?" asked Carlo of Maria, who was

sufficiently fond of Barker to not want to see him killed by a thug over drug money. And if she let Carlo gain the upper hand she knew she'd have no chance of claiming the money for herself.

Beyond Carlo, Barker was also distracted and confused, and not just because he was trying to figure out how to use a weapon he'd never held or even seen before. Crumpled on the road next to him, hidden from Maria's view behind the SUV, was Lucy Jones, who'd been at his side for most of the last few weeks since they met on board Starlight as it sailed across from Europe to spend the winter sailing around the Caribbean. Her job singing as part of the entertainment team had been interrupted after they'd met by the pool and people had started dying at the hands of, as it turned out, Barker's supposedly-dead wife Laura. Amid that chaos Lucy had discovered that her estranged father Aidan was a majority shareholder in the company that owned Galaxy Cruise Line and, using that position, was also involved in drug dealing that connected him with Ernesto Gutierrez. Unfortunately for Aidan, that relationship had led to his lifeless body currently lying in the boot of the black SUV after he, independently of Maria, had also been trying to find the cash that Barker had hidden in the storage unit. There hadn't recently been much love lost between father and daughter, but seeing him in the back of a car with a bullet-hole in his forehead made Lucy's brain stop functioning and gravity had taken over. There were no tears, just a blank stare of incomprehension.

Barker was torn. His instinct to console and protect Lucy was being overridden by the threat from the arrival of Gutierrez and Carlo just minutes ago. His mind was switching between helping her up and aiming the rifle at Carlo, who he'd seen reaching for his gun. He knew he only had one chance to gain the upper hand, or at least not lose the opportunity to defend

9

themselves. The few seconds of noise when the car hit the back of the Jaguar had only made the situation more surreal, and the stand-off that had appeared to be forming was added to when Maria jumped out of the Corolla and aimed her weapon at Carlo. It would've been comical if it wasn't so serious.

"Maria?" said Barker, swinging the rifle away from Carlo to point at Maria, then back again when he realised she wasn't aiming at him, "What's happening?"

"It's OK John. See to Lucy. I'm in control here."

Barker was about to turn to Lucy and help her stand up when Stephen, the father of one of Laura's other victims, stood up from his cover behind the car door and pointed at a spot in front of the Corolla and just to the right of the Jaguar. On the ground, lying at several unnatural angles was the body of Ernesto Gutierrez who had only seconds ago been standing proudly in front of his own vehicle when Maria had driven hers into the back of it. The low front of the Jaguar had pushed Gutierrez sharply in the back of the calves, collapsing him backwards onto the bonnet and scooping him up into the air. Judging by the blood next to his head and the angle of his neck to his shoulders, he had landed on his head on the tarmac. His eyes were open but nobody was home.

Barker, Carlo, Stephen and Maria stood looking in silence at the body, at each other, then back to Gutierrez again. Lucy couldn't see from her seat on the ground behind the SUV and had another dead body to think about. All three drawn weapons wilted in the hands of their holders as each of them seemed to instinctively realise that without the reason they all shared for being there, they no longer needed to use them. After nearly half a minute silently staring in contemplation of the gravity of what had happened, and exchanging concerned looks, Carlo and Maria appeared to have the same thought at the same time and looked at one another, down at the body, then at each other again.

At exactly the same moment they both said, "...Ricardo."

Chapter 3

Oblivious to what was going on in the road, Lucy vomited onto the tarmac in front of her and hung her head between her knees. Barker put the rifle back into the boot of the SUV, moving the blanket that had been hiding Aidan's body so that it now covered up both. He squatted down next to Lucy and put his hand on her shoulder. She sat upright and stared into the space in front of her. Still no tears...or words.

"I'm sorry," said Barker.

Lucy just shook her head, hitched up her knees and used her arms to push herself up onto her feet. "It's his own fault. It's what happens if you live in this world for too long."

Barker attempted to give her a hug to acknowledge her pain but she gasped and pushed him away. When he looked at her face she was staring over his shoulder at Carlo and Maria who had appeared behind him. Not having seen what had happened, Lucy was unaware of the scenario unfolding for them all.

"It's OK," said Barker, turning to look at Carlo and Maria and then back to Lucy, "Well...not OK, but they're not going to hurt us. Gutierrez is gone."

Lucy's expression was confused as she tried to comprehend what was going on and understand the new dynamics. Nobody here had ever been through anything quite like this before but they were going to have to deal with it as best they could. To make things even less clear Stephen Mitchell appeared next to Carlo.

"It's done," Stephen said, looking at Maria and then at the blanketed bundle in the back of the SUV.

"*What's* done?" said Barker.

"We have to get out of here fast," said Maria, "And get rid of as much...evidence as possible. Ernesto is back in his car." The pieces of the jigsaw fell together in Barker's brain as he saw Maria's eyebrow raise as she looked him right in the eye. They needed Aidan's body.

"Maria," said Carlo pointing at the holdalls on the ground, "We can fit more bags in the car. I'll put these in now."

"We're taking the money?" said Barker.

"Not all of it, just what we can grab. Come on, I'll help," said Maria, wanting to see the cash, but also to get Lucy out of the way so she wouldn't see what was happening to Aidan.

"Is that really important right now?"

"John, once we leave here we can never come back. This is the only chance we have. There will be people crawling all over here soon and they will find it."

Barker scowled knowing Maria was right and held Lucy as the three of them walked back into the unit via the fire door they'd come out of earlier.

Carlo and Stephen waited a few seconds before uncovering Aidan and lifting him up and out of the vehicle and across the road to the side of the Jaguar. They bundled him into the passenger seat next to Gutierrez and closed the door. They'd been lucky so far that no-one had come to investigate the noise of the crash. Being around the back of the building had given them some time but it wouldn't be much longer. They needed to move fast. Carlo ran back to the SUV and searched in the boot, pulling out a small fuel container and a clean cotton cloth. He walked over to the side of the Jaguar and casually opened the fuel flap pouring some petrol down the side of the bodywork as he tipped it up into the neck of the filler tube. He took a cigarette lighter out of his pocket and lit a corner of the cloth, making sure it caught properly before stuffing it into the tube next to the glugging container and waving at Stephen to get into the SUV.

A few seconds later Barker, Maria and a still-stunned Lucy emerged from the fire door of the building, having grabbed one more bag each and put the combination lock back on the storage unit door behind them. Carlo ushered them into the car, threw the remaining bags into the boot and covered them with the blood-stained blanket.

"Quickly. We have no time," urged Carlo.

Once they were all inside Carlo jumped into the driver's seat, hit the ignition button and drove away as calmly and calmly as possible given that he knew what was about to happen. Before they had travelled a hundred meters an almighty boom shook the car and lit up the rear-view mirror. Both Jaguar and Corolla and the bodies inside them were engulfed in flames.

Chapter 4

Five minutes later Carlo turned a corner slowly and parked the SUV down a side street, outside a cafe in the main part of town near the port. Barker wasn't happy at being so conspicuous but Carlo assured him it was better to stop somewhere full of tourists than locals because they would take no notice of them as they all climbed out and sat at a table outside where they could keep an eye on the car with the expensive cargo.

All five felt the need for alcohol to settle their nerves before deciding on their next move. The short drive from the storage unit had been done in stunned silence. It wasn't that there was nothing to talk about, but that nobody knew where to begin.

As they sat down Maria placed a mobile phone in the middle of the table. They all looked at it but nobody spoke for a few seconds.

"Who's Ricardo?" asked Barker, suddenly remembering what had been said outside the unit.

Maria and Carlo sat up straighter at the mention of the name and paused before explaining.

"Gutierrez's son," said Maria finally. Barker took a deep breath, slowly realising that the rest of this conversation wasn't going to be easy.

"He texts or rings his father twice a day, morning and evening, same times," said Carlo.

"What for?" Stephen asked, hoping it wasn't the obvious answer.

"To make sure he's still alive," said Carlo. Stephen sighed.

"How long now?" said Maria.

"Seven minutes."

A waiter interrupted their contemplation, asking what they would like to drink. Lucy asked for water but Barker asked for an extra brandy hoping she would drink it. The others ordered bottled beer or red wine.

"What happens in seven minutes?" said Barker when the waiter had gone.

"The countdown begins," replied Maria.

"Countdown?"

"Yes. The countdown to Ricardo finding out what has happened to his father. He will come looking."

"Not yet," said Carlo shaking his head, "He will send some of his men first."

"Aren't you one of his men?" said Lucy with an exhausted scowl, feeling like there was nothing much to gain by being polite. Her face had drained of colour.

"No." Carlos gave Lucy a resigned smile, "I see why you would think that, but I was employed by Mr Gutierrez as his bodyguard. Of course, I do other things sometimes but not for Ricardo."

"But you're still a killer."

Barker put his hand on Lucy's but she pulled it away.

"It's OK, I understand what you think about me. I am not an assassin. My job is protection if you understand the difference. I am paid to protect my employer. Today I failed."

The waiter returned with a tray of drinks and placed them

one by one on the table during the awkward silence.

"I didn't kill your father," Carlo continued when the waiter had gone, looking directly at Lucy, "That will have been Ricardo's men. He does the dirty work. He enjoys it."

The tension around the table was palpable. Each of them had at some point had a reason, either professional or personal, to hate or fear at least one of the others. But the bubble had been burst by the death of the man who had brought them all here and now taken their reasons away with him. Barker and Lucy had escaped first Maria, then Gutierrez. Maria had stayed alive long enough to find the money she'd been chasing Barker for. Stephen had helped get rid of a drug boss as some kind of indirect payback for the murder of his son by Laura, Barker's wife, in Gibraltar almost a fortnight ago. And Carlo had found himself looking for a change of career. But they all now seemed to be facing a new shared threat.

"OK, so what do we do now?" said Stephen, voicing what everyone else was thinking.

"We have to kill him," stated Maria matter-of-factly, "If we don't we all die."

With the exception of Carlo who just nodded imperceptibly, everyone looked at Maria in stunned silence, like they must've misheard what she'd said. Maria continued with the explanation she knew they were waiting for.

"We just killed his father...I just killed his father. So that's me at the top of the hit list. Carlo let it happen on duty, so he's dead too. John and Lucy stole millions of dollars from him...at least that's how he sees it. And Stephen, I'm sorry, you were with me. You saw what happened. They can't let that go."

Stephen's expression remained remarkably unchanged considering the news.

"He's in charge now," Carlo continued, looking at the others, "His father's death puts him at the top. But he has to be seen to be strong otherwise rivals will think he is weak. He has to act quickly."

"Won't killing him just create a vacuum for someone else to take over?" said Stephen, breaking the silence from the others.

"Yes, but that's the only way we survive," said Maria.

"I don't follow."

"If...*when* Ricardo goes there will be a vacuum as you say, but then there is no more family to take over. His men will turn on each other or go looking for work elsewhere. The rival gangs will fight over the business. It will be horrible. But it won't involve us. They won't care about who killed Ernesto. Just that he's gone, along with his son. And they won't even know about the money. We'll all be off the hook. Except maybe Carlo."

Carlo gave Maria a confused look, "What do you mean?"

"Well like you said, you just failed in your duty to protect your boss. It's unlikely that will stay a secret between us. Word travels fast. You're not going to walk into another job in another firm. At the very least you'll be demoted to being a regular thug. Better to look for a new line of work I think."

Carlo just shrugged.

"I'm not happy about this. I'm a policeman. We put people in jail, not kill them," said Barker, being the voice of reason.

"You don't have the luxury of choice, John. It's as if he is standing here in front of you right now. You have a gun, he has a gun. One of you is going to die. What are you going to do?"

"Shoot him in the leg and put him in jail."

"Do you think jail makes a difference to someone like Ricardo? Come on John, you've seen the movies. You know he'd be even more powerful inside prison. It's the safest place he could possibly be. He'd be pulling the strings wherever you went and you'd still die...Lucy too."

"Why can't we just disappear?" said Lucy, "I mean we have the money, don't we?"

"For the same reason. He will find you. Money has a smell, Lucy. These people are able to follow it wherever it goes. Besides, do you want to live your life like that? Looking over your shoulder, wondering if he's onto you yet? It would only be a matter of time."

The table went quiet again as each of them sipped their drink and thought about what Maria and Carlo had said, and what lay ahead for them.

The phone pinged and made them jump out of their daze:

Hola papá, ¿estás bien? ¿Encontraste lo que buscabas?

Hey Dad, are you okay? Did you find what you were looking for?

Chapter 5

RICARDO

I should have gone with him but he wouldn't let me. 'Carlo will look after me,' he said, 'Like always.' Carlo is his favourite. I guess you learn to trust someone and then rely on them. But why not me? Anyway, it's only been five minutes so I'm worrying for nothing. It's just that he usually texts right back. His phone is always in his pocket. Or in Carlo's pocket. I'll track it.

He was out chasing that Englishman and his girlfriend over money. He didn't let me get involved. Said it wasn't worth my time, an easy one. He was having fun. I think he'll retire soon. He wants a quiet life, no more drama. Just a few more pay days to feather the nest a bit more then he'll pick one of his homes and move away and leave things to me. He tried to get me to leave the business once. After bringing me up in that environment and getting me used to that world, that violence, and making me prove myself. Then he tells me I should leave. Is he worried about me, about my future, or does he not think I'm capable? It just made me more determined to prove I could do it. To have the life that he has. Now I'm committed to it I'm not going back.

I'm calling him. He hates that in the day time, in case he's in the middle of business. So I message in the day and ring at night, when he's home. But it's eight minutes now and no reply, which is unheard of, so I don't care...I'm dialling...

Nothing. It's ringing out. If he's there and doesn't want disturbing he might cut me off early anyway. But I can't leave a message. You don't leave voicemail messages for a cartel boss even if he is your father. Far too risky. Thirty seconds and it's still ringing. This isn't good. I'll send somebody once I pin down the location. I'd go myself but he forbids that. You can't have the current boss and the next boss running into the same trouble and both of us getting mixed up in it. He won't even let me go in the same car with him any more in case it gets blown up or shot at. 'Who will avenge me if we both die?' he said. He's been scared like that since the death of my brother Roberto.

His phone was last located at an industrial estate out of town. Google maps tells me it's a...self storage company. That makes sense. Twenty million in cash would take up a lot of space, but it's hardly the most secure. Still, hiding in plain sight is always a good move. Maybe this English cop is smart. Wait...this was half an hour ago. He never stays in one place that long, not outside of our properties at least.

What's that? A text! It must be him. No, wait, it's from Julio. One word. A code word...

The *code word...* Muerte

Chapter 6

"Carlo, you did turn off the GPS on his phone right?" asked Maria as she read the text from Ricardo.

"Yes of course," replied Carlo, rolling his eyes, "He will track it to the unit but no further. But we need to move."

"Can't you just answer him?" said Barker, "Buy us some time?"

"I'm afraid not John," said Maria, "They use code words. They have a kind of family language of their own, maybe a dialect from their home village from years ago. Sometimes they would use it in front of me if they were talking business. They didn't completely trust anyone outside the family."

"What are we going to do with the car?" said Stephen.

"We have to empty it, hide the bags," said Carlo, "I know a place, a safe place, but we must split up. We can't be seen together any more. People will start to ask questions."

"So you're going to disappear by yourself with the money?" said Barker, raising his eyebrows.

Carlo closed his eyes and took a deep breath in and out, "I know we don't all trust each other. And maybe that was right at one time, but if we don't work together now we are all in trouble. One of you should come with me. How about you?"

"I'll go," said Lucy.

"No. What?...Are you sure?" said Barker, seeing the serious-ness of Lucy's expression.

"Yes. I need to do something. I want to be busy. Otherwise my brain might explode."

Barker wasn't happy letting Lucy out of his sight but knew he couldn't stop her.

"So where do we meet?" said Stephen, "I mean, if we're going to do this, shouldn't we be in control?"

"There's only one place we can be in control," said Maria, "This is their territory but on board the ship we have the advantage. We've all been inside...and John and Lucy know it much better than any of us. That's where it should be."

"Well we both work there, but how are you all going to get back on board?" said Barker.

"I'm booked on for the next ten days, back to Florida then out to the Caribbean. I'm hoping I'll need the holiday."

"Officially I haven't left yet," said Stephen, "But I'm cutting it fine. They'll be checking my cabin any time soon, so I'll have to see if they'll let me stay."

"It won't be a problem," said Lucy, "It's not full. You'll all get something. Let's go."

Carlo stood up and motioned to Lucy to walk to the car with him. He asked the others not to all leave at once, but Maria and Stephen chose to leave together as the convincing couple again and walked around the corner out of sight. Barker sat for a minute realising he'd been left with the bill, so he swallowed his brandy and winced before leaving the cash on the table and headed across the road towards the port.

A steady stream of people were still leaving Starlight having made the most of their final free breakfast before disembarking and wheeling their own cases down the gangway and out of the port gates. As he walked in the opposite direction to them, back towards the ship, Barker thought how lucky they were to not have any clue what was going on in his world and wondered if one day he and Lucy might enjoy a holiday like they'd just had, without all the danger and drama. Just maybe not on a cruise ship.

Halfway between the gates and the ship he was taken aback by the familiar face coming towards him and slowed down a little, unsure what to do or say. The last time he'd seen this man was when he'd been betrayed by him, leading him straight into Ernesto Gutierrez's clutches.

When they were about twenty meters away from each other Ashton recognised him and instinctively stopped in his tracks, equally unsure about what to do next. His wife Patricia was walking next to him pushing their daughter Melissa in her buggy. Barker approached him slowly. Ashton asked his wife to continue walking and wait at the gates where they would pick up a taxi.

"John, I'm sorry..."

"It's OK Ashton. I understand."

"My family. I had to..."

"I know. He told me."

"Ernesto?"

"Yes."

"I...I'm glad you're OK."

"He's dead."

Ashton's mouth opened but no words came out. He seemed genuinely relieved that although he had been used by Gutierrez while he was on holiday with his family, to trick Barker into leading him to the money, Barker had not only survived but seemingly come out on top. "It's over?"

"Not yet. He has family. It will be over tomorrow. One way or another."

A car horn beeped twice from outside the gates. Ashton looked up to see his wife waving from the door of a taxi, having picked up Melissa and loaded the buggy into the boot. "I have to go John. I'm sorry...good luck."

"You too Ashton. You too."

Chapter 7

BARKER

Barker walked into his cabin with a strong feeling in his stomach that this could be his last day on this ship. Maybe any cruise ship. Right now he thought that was almost certainly a good thing, but it would depend on what Lucy wanted to do with her future and if he was going to be a part of it. If this really could end today, and even if it ended well, she could go back to what she loved and continue working on cruise ships, and he could continue working for the cruise line security team as he'd been invited to do by the captain. They could see enough of each other to start a proper relationship until he was transferred to another ship, which was highly likely given the brief he'd been given to improve safety across the fleet. But he didn't know if that's what he, or she, wanted.

Being with Lucy would be the only good thing to come out of the mess of these last three weeks of trauma and confusion. It was what had kept them both going. The thought of being able to bring it all to an end right now, today, was intoxicating, but it required the one thing he couldn't countenance bringing himself to do...taking someone's life, or at least allowing someone else to do it. Even someone like Ricardo's.

The logic was clear. If they got rid of him (*'got rid' - there's a euphemism if ever there was one,* he thought.) then it would be over. Nobody else had any reason to come after them once the Gutierrez family was taken out of the equation. And he couldn't deny that Maria was right when she said they had no choice, that if they didn't remove Ricardo from the situation he would eventually come after each and every one of them until they were all dead. Surely they could capture him and hand him over to the police, make sure he was jailed and held securely, in solitary if necessary? At one time he'd have trusted his old colleagues to do exactly that but he'd been betrayed by Rob, his old boss, who'd thrown him into this mess in the beginning, and then by Ashton from the local police. It seemed Gutierrez had fingers in every pie.

Can you reason with a cartel boss? Unlikely at the best of times. Impossible when you've just killed his father. He hadn't killed him though, had he? Maria had. But she'd been helping him get away from Gutierrez and hadn't intended to kill anyone. Had she? That surely wouldn't wash with Ricardo anyway, and he couldn't really betray Maria who he knew wasn't really on his side, but had just saved both his and Lucy's lives.

Besides, Barker was in possession of a large amount of cash which Ernesto claimed had originally belonged to him before it had passed through several pairs of dirty hands, and was just about to retrieve when Maria's foot hit the throttle pedal. Ricardo would know that. Could they just give it to him as blood money? Could he trust Ricardo even if he accepted it? Unlikely. He would take the money and then kill them all later. That's how it works. That's why cartels are successful. They solve problems by eliminating them even if the problem is a person. And now Barker found himself in that situation with apparently only one reliable solution.

Maybe there was another way. Maybe if Ricardo could be provoked into attacking first, Barker thought, he could fight back in self-defence. Would that make him feel any better about it? To some extent but it was high risk. It meant letting Ricardo get close enough to get a jump on him before he made his own move. That could go either way. Ricardo was used to doing things like this, at least more than he was. A silent shot, a knife in the back, a blunt instrument to the head. He didn't even know what Ricardo looked like, so how would he know he was coming? Carlo and Maria could tell him what he looked like, but unless you've seen a person for yourself you'd always be one step slower until it was too late. And he might not even do it himself. Why wouldn't he send his thugs to do his dirty work? That way he wouldn't risk being caught.

And then there was Laura. Could he do it for her? Was Ricardo responsible for the attack that sent her over the edge and turned her into a killer? She'd said it was because she was working for the forensic team investigating a drug deal gone wrong in London. Ricardo probably didn't think twice about sending a team to try to kill her. But they'd failed and only succeeded in driving her to murder those she felt should pay – the relatives of the shipping company directors. It wasn't lost on Barker that if she'd died she wouldn't have had the chance to kill all those innocent people, and then been hunted down and killed for her crimes. One way or another her fate had been sealed at that point in time. So maybe there was a reason for him to do it after all.

Chapter 8

LUCY

Right now Lucy was in no doubt she would kill Ricardo if she got half a chance, having just seen her father's dead body in the boot of the car, put there by one of Ricardo's men if he didn't do it himself. She might die trying but at least she would feel like she'd made an effort to put some things right.

Carlo was beside her driving that very car with her father's body replaced by half a dozen holdalls packed full of hundred dollar bills. She should have been scared, terrified, of being there in that situation, but it was all so surreal. A group of people from opposing sides who once had a problem with one or more of the others, suddenly relieved of those problems and given another shared one by a freak accident. If it was an accident? Lucy couldn't know yet whether Maria had meant to kill Ernesto. What did she expect when she drove her car into his? But if Maria hadn't turned up when she did, she and Barker could be dead by now, 'sleeping with the fishes' or whatever they said in The Godfather. It had been Lucy's idea to get Stephen to persuade Maria to help. She knew Maria had fallen out with Ernesto and that she was motivated by money – the thought of getting her hands on the cash would be sure to pique her interest. And despite betraying him more than once (not to mention shooting Lucy in the leg) Maria had a thing for Barker. Not that kind of 'thing', but she liked him and didn't want him to become another of the Gutierrez family's victims. She'd just gone too far and made it worse instead of better.

Lucy however, did have a thing for Barker. Her stomach flipped as she thought back to the first time they met in the sun by the pool on the Lido deck just a couple of days into the Atlantic crossing, when he spilled her drink down her cleavage before everything went pear-shaped. And then when they thought it was all over when they got off the ship in Nassau, she sat in hospital for a week nursing a bullet wound. He'd visited every day, twice a day, bringing magazines to ease the boredom, and guilty-pleasure snacks to compensate for bland hospital food. And then the night they'd spent together at that posh hotel, awkwardly discovering just how much they felt, and fell, for each other. *One bloody night, she thought.* Then he'd got himself kidnapped and they'd ended up in this mess. How could she feel so much for a man who had brought nothing but trouble into her life? But he obviously cared for her so much, and that had been lacking in her life for too long. Maybe she couldn't risk trying and dying. Not unless he was in trouble. She had too much to live for.

She wondered why she had volunteered to chaperone the money and accompany Carlo to wherever he planned to hide it. At the cafe it had been barely half an hour after finding her dad and she'd not cared about what anyone said or did, or what they wanted to do. She'd wanted to do something, anything, preferably dramatic, to make a difference to the day. But now she was coming out of that red mist back into the real world and wondering if she'd made a wise choice. Carlo was a paid thug after all. A particularly charming and attractive one she had to admit, but still a thug. No doubt he had blood on his hands like the others, but loyalties were all mixed up right now and she would play along as much as she could until it seemed too dangerous. She thought she would soon know if he wasn't going to play ball, and could make a scene to get some attention.

It looked like they were heading to the port like all the others. In fact, that was Stephen and Maria they passed walking along the road in the same direction, looking for all the world like a married couple on holiday for their anniversary. Where could Carlo be thinking of hiding just over ten million in cash at the port? Was that a smart decision? She didn't know any more. He pulled the car over by the building where she'd met Ashton that day when Barker had disappeared, and they'd later been rescued by Laura.

"I have to make a call," Carlo said as he turned off the engine.

Chapter 9

CARLO

Of all those involved in the death of his boss, Carlo was the most confident of surviving the day. Physically there were few people he was afraid of, and of course he knew Ricardo. He didn't like him, but he knew him. He knew what a sneaky little bastard he could be. That was what scared Carlo. Ricardo wouldn't play by the rules. It wouldn't be a fair fight. He might not even show up, let his men do the work for him instead. Maybe that's how the bosses got to the top and stayed there. That was basically his job working for Ernesto, but he'd graduated to being his bodyguard, which still required some dirty work now and then but not unless absolutely necessary. The only downside was, when they asked you did it, or it would be you they did it to.

Maybe now he would have that choice. To continue or not. The money was good but the risks were real. Once you're in it you can't get out. Not alive anyway. You're in for life, yours or the boss's. Then you have a chance. *This is my chance,* he thought. He hadn't chosen this life for himself. His brother had dragged him into it for the money. He'd been bigger and fitter than his brother so they both knew he'd be good at it. He didn't have much of an education but he wasn't stupid. Growing up with a father in prison they'd learned to be smart and look after themselves. When he found he could earn good money easily by being loyal to the right people he didn't see the point in staying at school. He wished his brother had done though. He might still be alive today.

I have millions of dollars in the back of this car, thought Carlo, *I could just disappear.* He could pull over, push Lucy out of the door (she wouldn't put up much of a fight) and drive away, steal a boat and disappear. The only things that were stopping him were the thought of his girlfriend and a small streak of decency inside him, plus the fear that Ricardo would find him eventually, even if he found a remote island in the middle of the Atlantic to live on, where you couldn't spend any of the money. No, there was no option. The only way to enjoy even a share of it was to make sure Ricardo was no longer a problem.

Could he trust the others though? Especially a cop. No, Maria was the one to watch. He'd seen her work her way into Ernesto's life only recently and then try to betray him when she thought she could have the money to herself. She was lucky to be alive after Ernesto had dismissed her. He still didn't know how she'd got away with that. But now that she was here and involved, he had to keep her on side and keep an eye on her. *Keep your friends close and your enemies closer*, they say. They all wanted the same thing – Ricardo out of the picture – but what happens after that?

And what happens now? Would they all look to him, being the so-called professional? Surely he couldn't rely on Lucy, as fired up as she was about her dad being killed. Ricardo would swat her like a fly. And Barker, the cop? Could he help dispose of Ricardo? Carlo doubted his motivation. He was the least likely to do something like that. Maria yes, definitely, but he knew little about Stephen. He looked like he could mean business. Why was he involved otherwise? We will find out once we get rid of this money.

Chapter 10

MARIA

The walk back along the coast road to the cruise port with Stephen had made Maria feel something she hadn't felt for a long time. Not that she was interested in him. He seemed like her type: handsome, intelligent, with a mysterious side, but he wasn't from her world. Although maybe that was a good thing? *I felt normal for a few minutes*, she thought to herself as she let herself into her suite that was just as she'd left it that morning when he'd waited for her outside but pretended he'd bumped into each her by accident. She hadn't felt that for a long time, since she'd first met Michael Brennan, before she realised what he was involved with and ended up in jail.

Maria made herself a gin and tonic from the mini-bar and sat on the balcony overlooking the port and the town, reflecting on the last few weeks, months and years. She thought about her daughter in hiding from the violent world Maria had found herself in, and about Julio, her son, who she'd lost to that world. She remembered the reason she'd come on the cruise in the first place – to avenge Julio by finding Michael. He was back in prison where he belonged and Vega, the man Michael had sent to kill her, was dead at her own hand. So finishing the job with

Ricardo held no fear for her. But it wouldn't be half as easy.

Ricardo had tried to pick up Maria in the bar where she first met Ernesto. She had even contemplated amusing him for a while until she realised he wasn't the main man. Ever since then, Ricardo had never liked her. He saw her as a rival for Ernesto's attention. *So immature*, she thought. He remained polite of course because his father demanded it but now he was gone that pretence would come crashing down. He would like nothing more than to make her history. He'd failed to do that once before when he'd handed to job over to someone else who had seriously underestimated her survival instincts.

And what about the money? Wasn't that why she was still here? It had just been a bonus at first when she discovered Michael was prying it out of Aidan's hands, and then Barker took it from her which only made her want it more. She had even managed to earn the trust of Ernesto in order to help her get to it, once she found out he'd supplied Aidan with the goods he traded to get it.

That money would buy her and her daughter a new life, but right now it looked like she might have to share it. Could she deal with that or would she have to fight for it again? Carlo might be hard to deal with for obvious reasons. She shuddered at the thought she'd let him drive away with it all in the back of a car. At least Lucy was with him to supervise, but did she trust her either? She knew she wouldn't go anywhere without Barker. They would make a good couple. They were normal people who would be happy with a normal life just being together. They might not even want to touch the money. Knowing Barker he would hand it over to the authorities wherever he ended up, so she knew she had to prevent him from having control over it.

She liked Barker, for reasons she couldn't completely explain.

He was certainly not her type, but he represented a world she realised she probably should be part of. A good, honest world of work and reward. His reward was Lucy. He had lost people like everyone else and deserved something out of all this.

So would she have to be the one to organise what came next? She and Carlo knew the Gutierrez family best, how they would behave. Barker sounded reluctant to get involved although he was in it just as deep as everyone else. Lucy would stand by him...or maybe take the lead. She'd lost her father after all. What about Stephen? She hadn't known him long, barely a few half-hours shared in specific circumstances, almost scripted for them. There was a lot about him she didn't know, and she didn't really have the time to find out. In the car earlier he had opened up about losing his son, killed by Barker's wife. That must have been difficult. So he had the same level of motivation as everyone else to see this brought to an end. But who was going to actually do it? And how?

Chapter 11

STEPHEN

I need a drink, Stephen thought, as he walked off the gangway into the Atrium on Deck Five. Out of politeness, he had asked Maria if she wanted to join him in a small bar upstairs where one waiter was serving the few people left on board on what was disembarkation day for everyone else. He was relieved when she said no, thank you. She was clearly a beautiful and interesting woman and there were a lot of deep and dark details to be discovered about her in another time and place, but not right here, right now. Now he had to sit and think about what had happened this morning and what his options and motivations were.

When he had agreed to help Lucy with her backup plan to persuade Maria to help her and Barker escape from Ernesto, he had no idea it could end up like this, with his life on the line. None of the others could have predicted it either. But then this wasn't the first time he'd faced this kind of danger.

His main worry was Josh, his grandson. He had lost his dad Jack in Gibraltar on that horrible day. Not only lost him, but had seen it happen. That was never going to leave him. How does a child make any sense of that? How could he have allowed himself to come to the other side of the world and leave Josh at a time like this? That was another selfish thing he'd done. He had his mum Katie and all her family of course. He wasn't lacking in love and care. But he should be there too. Right now he wished he was.

But what's done is done and he didn't have a lot of choice at this moment in time. He could help make the world a slightly better place by removing one very bad person from it, even if someone else would soon take his place. He'd done it before, but that was a long time ago, and back then it had been his job.

It might not even come down to him. Carlo looked like he could handle it. So did Maria for that matter. But he had no idea who Ricardo was or how he would behave. They could all be biting off a lot more than they could chew in thinking they could get the better of him. One thing was for certain...it was going to be sorted in less than twenty-four hours. Starlight was due to sail in the early afternoon, repositioning to Florida, with hardly any passengers on board – just those who were booked on the following cruise south into the Caribbean. Ricardo couldn't let them get that far. He would have to come for them before the ship got to Florida and they disappeared. He wouldn't want the inconvenience of having to go and look for them when right now he had them all in the palm of his greasy little hand.

How would Ricardo know where to find them? Not difficult really. Carlo would just turn that phone back on and let him track it. But Ricardo knew about Barker and the money, and if there was one thing a man like that could do, it was to follow the trail of money. He would know that Barker and Lucy would come back here. It was where they felt safest. But not for long.

Chapter 12

The half-hour after boarding Starlight felt like being in limbo for Barker. He'd agreed with Stephen and Maria that they'd wait until Carlo and Lucy were safely on board before they got together to talk about their next move. He knew he really should report to the captain to update him on his findings on the short cruise they'd just finished, about the procedures for boarding passengers and loading/unloading products on and off the ship, but he'd not had time to prepare anything with all the extra-curricular activity of last night, so he held out for now and watched the crew doing a lifeboat drill a few decks below his window.

A knock at the door woke him from his daydream and he got up and looked through the peephole into the corridor outside. It was Lucy. He quickly opened the door and ushered her inside, giving her a hug before she could say anything.

"You're OK?" said Barker.

"Fine," Lucy replied.

"Where did you go?"

"Not far."

"Where did you leave the bags?"

"Best you don't know."

"Really?" Barker sounded a little offended.

"Yes, but suffice to say it was close by and it's safe."

"It won't be close by when we get to Florida."

"Trust me, John, it's safe. Anything happened here?"

"No, but now that you're both back we'll have to make plans. Do we know where everyone is?"

"Carlo told me his room number. Stephen knows where Maria's room is. But I saw him in the bar when we boarded. He said he'd wait there for us.

Barker was a bit surprised by this new Lucy. She was colder, almost blunt, and had lost her smile. But he knew had had to cut her some slack like she had with him. This morning she'd followed him off the ship, not knowing if either of them would make it through the day, or even the morning. They managed the latter, but then she had found her dad's body in the boot of a car, which would change anyone, at least for a while. She'd been there for him when Laura turned up, and even stuck with him when he'd followed Laura to the lighthouse before the end came for her. There were too many endings happening all at once. Hopefully, today would bring things to an end for all of them, but in a good way.

Chapter 13

When Lucy and Barker got to the bar on Deck Six, they found Carlo and Maria had joined Stephen at a table in the corner furthest from the counter so no-one could overhear their conversation, but within sight of the gangway onto Deck Five they'd entered through. The last few stragglers were disembarking with their wheeled suitcases humming along the marble floor, then bumping onto the gangway itself and disappearing into the sunshine outside. There were few new passengers boarding today, but many of the thousand or so who would be continuing to Florida tonight had got off the ship early to spend the morning in Nassau before returning in a couple of hours for an early-afternoon sail-away.

"Is there somewhere we can watch that doorway without being seen?" said Maria to Barker as he sat down next to her at the table. "And what about the cargo doors?"

"Yes," he said, "I can go to the security office and log on to the camera feed from there and watch it. I can start from when we got here and speed it up a bit until I've caught up. The cargo doors are closed now. There wasn't much to load for a one day trip. They'll top up in Florida. Can you show me what I'm looking for?"

Maria took her phone from her pocket and scrolled through a

gallery of photos going back a couple of months to a gathering that included Ernesto and Ricardo, arms round each other's shoulders, beaming into the camera as if they were any ordinary father and son, and not the head of, and heir to, a drug dealing dynasty.

"I remember that," Carlo interrupted, "Your father was there too," he said, looking at Lucy, who stared back at him without saying a word.

Barker took the phone from Maria and zoomed into the image so Ricardo's face filled the frame. He was just like his father, only thinner, less rounded by the effects of a life of plenty. He had dark, almost black straight hair, floppy on top but cropped at the sides. Not a good looking man considering his youth. Maybe that didn't help with his disposition.

"Girlfriend?" said Barker at random, passing the phone to Lucy so she would know what he looked like too.

"Rarely," said Maria, "And usually paid for one way or another. We were never really sure. Ernesto wondered about him, thought he might not like women if you know what I mean. But it's difficult to find love in their world. Some know who you are and want your money..."

"Like you?" interrupted Lucy.

Maria paused and smiled calmly, "Yes Lucy, like me, but I made a bad choice and lost a son to this life and want something back from it. For the daughter that I had to hide." Lucy looked down at the table, embarrassed. "The women that don't know who these men are usually run scared when they find out, or try to stick it out for a while, but they never last. Again, like me."

"You don't really think he's going to walk through the front door though do you?" said Stephen, "He knows that you two would recognise him. Or is he that brazen?"

"He is brazen," said Carlo, "But I don't think he'll announce his arrival like that. He'll know we are watching. But he might send others that way, people we don't know, who can help him. But of course, they could already be on board. We really can't trust anyone."

"You can turn the location back on Ernesto's phone now," said Maria, "So he will know where we are, or at least where the phone is."

"Already done it," said Carlo, "I did it as soon as we got on board. But he will know we are here anyway. Where else would we go? We couldn't hide on the island forever."

"I agree," said Stephen, "We all have reason to want this finished. We could run but he'd find us and we'd never know when. The question is how we go about it. Shouldn't we have some sort of plan?"

"The first stage is to get him on board. By sail-away in a couple of hours, we can assume he is here. Then we will have to lure him out and trap him again. You two know this ship better than us," Carlo looked at Barker and Lucy, "Where do you think we can do that?"

Lucy and Barker looked at each other and both said, "In plain sight." Lucy continued, "This place is huge and it's a warren of rooms and passageways. There are a million places to hide. The best scenario would be if we see him arrive and can keep track of him, find out where his room is and watch that."

"That's too simple Lucy," said Maria, "If I was him I wouldn't go near my room."

"What do you mean?" said Barker.

"Well it's too obvious, isn't it? He'd know we would find him easily, so he won't do that."

"He'll have to book a room to get on board."

"Yes, he'll have to book one, but he doesn't have to go in it. He'll stay well clear of it. It's only for the one night and it's not like he'll have time to sleep unless he gets rid of all of us before bedtime. He's got work to do and it all has to be over by the time we dock tomorrow."

There was a brief silence as Maria's words sank in. This would all be over by the morning...one way or another.

"He has to come and look for us doesn't he?" said Lucy, "If he's going to get at any of us he first has to find us."

"But there's no point hiding away," said Stephen.

"I know. I'm not suggesting we do that. In fact, I'd suggest the opposite. I think once the ship sails we should all spread out and keep our eyes open for him, or for anything unusual happening. I also think we should have at least one other person within sight so that we can keep an eye out for each other and let each other know if we notice anything. We can swap around as we go from place to place. It means he can see us but we will see him, and it will draw him out into the open. It's the safest place to be."

The others nodded in agreement, a little surprised that it was the ship's singer who had come up with the plan, but happy to have a shared purpose again and the clarity to focus on it. Barker stood up and said to the table in general, "I'll watch the security cameras. You should go and eat. I think it's going to be a long day."

Chapter 14

RICARDO

I can't get close enough. The police and firefighters are all over the place right now, but I know my father is inside that burned-out wreck. He loved his car and he'd have to be dead to allow that to happen to it. Most people know who it belonged to. I can't think of many people who would be stupid enough to let this happen unless they had no choice. I can't get hold of Carlo, so either he's in there with him or he's responsible. Either way, he let my father die. Either way, he is a dead man.

There's another car in the back of it that I don't recognise. A hire car. I have people checking the plate already. Luckily the back end of it survived so I can read that from here. We can find out where it came from and question the rental company. They will have footage on their CCTV of who hired it. It can't be an accident, not here, at the dead-end of a road on an industrial estate next to a storage unit. Whoever has done this knew what they were doing. But then why did it go up in flames? That happens in the movies but not in real life. I should know. I've seen a few of these types of accidents myself. You have to make them happen.

Who would want him dead? Lots of people. Comes with the territory. But who is stupid enough to do it, right here, right now?

This isn't your usual hit. Too public. No, this happened in the heat of the moment. Something went wrong. That means they weren't professionals. Maybe it was that cop and his singer girlfriend who had the money my father kept talking about. But they wouldn't have killed him would they? In the open like this? They would at least know the consequences of that. It doesn't add up. Someone else is involved, and I have an idea who that might be. But I thought she was dead.

His phone! It's alive again. Have I got this all wrong? Could it be? Oh god, they're bringing bodies out of the car. That's him. That must be him. Where is it? Where is that phone? It can't be far away in that time. It's...It's at the port. It looks like it's in the water next to a jetty. Did they just throw it away? No wait, of course, what don't they show on a map of the port? What is in the water at the port? Ships, obviously. A ship. That ship.

So it is the cop and his girlfriend. But I know my father sent Carlo there to watch them for a few days too. It could be either. And she was on that ship too. Maria. It could be any of them. Whoever did it turned the phone off and back on again. They know what they're doing. They're taunting me. Do they not think I'm mad enough already? They kill my father and then do this? Maybe they're just stupid and don't realise what they've done? No. Why would they keep his phone unless they wanted to do this? Maybe they just tossed it in the water.

I'm going crazy. I have to calm down and think. I know where they are and I know what I have to do. Now I just have to do it. Word will get out soon if it hasn't already. The vultures can smell death and will be starting to circle around me soon. The only way to stop that is to make it clear what happens when you attack my family.

Chapter 15

Barker let himself into the security office with the contactless Sea Star device on his wrist. All the passengers had one to let them into their rooms and buy drinks and souvenirs from the shops, but his had been upgraded to allow him access to most of the crew-only areas around the ship. He acknowledged the couple of engineers inside who recognised him and smiled. He had just about become a familiar face on board in the few days since he'd been given an official position and was starting to feel like a member of the crew, albeit a nearly middle-aged white Englishman amongst a crew of mostly younger people from the Asia-Pacific regions. They'd all begun to accept him now and didn't question anything when he sat down at a hot-desk and tapped at the keyboard to log himself into the gangway CCTV.

He was able to find the feed and where the footage was being stored and start from when the doors opened first thing this morning. Speeding the footage up gradually, he skipped through the first few minutes until passengers could be seen to be disembarking with their luggage. The flow of bodies was all one-way. Nobody would be coming on board at that time. In fact, the crew had set up barriers to funnel people from the Atrium into the gangway to get people off as efficiently as possible. A long queue formed back into the ship but everyone seemed to be polite with each other and everything was going smoothly so he sped up the footage a bit more.

After a few minutes in real time, or about half an hour of speeded-up footage, Barker noticed the numbers thinning out. A minute or so later he saw that the crew had split the gangway barriers to allow a lane for people to get back on board – embarking either for the first time, or because they had gone into town earlier and were coming back. A couple of minutes later he saw a tall couple boarding and waving their own Sea Star bracelets at the sensors in the doorway. It was Maria and Stephen. Shortly after, he saw himself do the same thing and felt a shudder as he remembered he hadn't been with Lucy and that she had been somewhere 'close' with Carlo, hiding the money. He didn't really know what that meant but had other things to worry about now.

He slowed down the recorded footage a little so he could assess the arrivals to see if any could be Ricardo. He couldn't believe he would just walk straight in, but couldn't imagine how else he would get on board. Maybe he wouldn't turn up at all. Any of these people could be working for Ricardo and he would never know. There could be several of them. Then the footage flickered and slowed down and he realised he was watching the live feed. This was going to be a boring couple of hours unless he saw that face from Ernesto's phone peering at him from his monitor. But it was a crucial job to know where any threat might come from. It reminded him of his days in the police force, a lot of it spent watching and waiting for things to happen. A lot of the time nothing did. But he didn't think today was going to be one of those days. Today something was definitely going to happen, so he just hoped one of their group would see it coming.

Barker jumped out of his concentration as a hand tapped him on the shoulder. He'd heard the door open but just assumed it was one or other of the engineers going about their day and didn't look up. Lucy had obviously sneaked in at the same time. She pulled up a chair and sat beside him, placing a plate on the table in front of him, full of bits from the buffet on the Lido Deck – a couple of sandwiches and pieces of fruit. She put a mug of coffee down in front of him then put her arm around his back and squeezed him close to her.

"I'm sorry," she said.

"What for?" Barker replied, pressing the pause button on the video feed.

"Being distant."

"That's OK. I understand. You've had a bad day."

Lucy nodded. "And cryptic...about the money."

"Well you trust me, so I trust you."

Lucy kissed Barker on the cheek, "Will we get out of this John?"

"There are five of us. I fancy our chances."

"And what then?"

"What do you mean?"

"I mean what do *we* do then? What about us?"

Barker understood what she meant. They'd never really had this discussion before. "We do whatever we want do. Together... if that's what you want." Barker felt his face flush slightly.

"You know I do John. We've hardly been away from each other since you spilled that drink down my cleavage by the pool, just so you could get a closer look."

Barker smiled. "Apart from a couple of kidnappings and a week in hospital you mean?"

"It was worth it for that night in the hotel," Barker felt Lucy's hand on his thigh under the table," I want more of that John. I want to be with you. Please be careful today."

Barker sighed, "I will. And you too."

"Maria's a badass. So is Carlo. I'm sure they can handle this. And they know him. Stephen? Well, we don't know much about him but he seems to be on our side and looks like he's not afraid."

"I don't know why he's got himself involved this much."

"He lost his son to the Gutierrez family — indirectly at least. He's hurting and he wants to be able to do something about it. It will bring him some closure."

"I liked your plan by the way. I couldn't think of any other way."

"Thanks. I just thought it was better to be out there looking out for each other amongst the other guests than to hide away and not know what was going on. We should be proactive. I think we'll have to mix it up though."

"How do you mean?"

"I mean switch around throughout the day. I think it's best if one of us stays with one of them — me with Carlo, you with Maria. So they can alert us if they see him."

"I think Maria's taken."

"Yeah, they do seem to get on, don't they? That's my fault. I introduced them. Anyway, I have to go and tell the band that I've been projectile vomiting all morning."

"Have you?"

"No, but I can't possibly sing with them today, can I? I'm going to get into big trouble for that, but if this last couple of weeks has taught me anything it's that trouble is relative."

Chapter 16

In a side street just off the main road about half a mile from the port, a door round the back of a shop opened quietly and two people stepped out onto the pavement. One was a tall thin man with straight black hair, wearing baggy jeans and a leather jacket that had seen better days. Next to him was a serious-looking woman wearing ripped faded jeans, a red vest top and a white baseball cap. The man was Jose Ramirez, the chief engineer from Starlight, and the woman was Mary Tkachuk from the admin department. The shop they had just left via the fire escape was a jewellers. The same jewellers visited a few days ago by Eduardo Jiminez, who was later found face down in the dock behind Starlight's hull.

"What that a wise move Jose?" said Mary.

"What? Stripping the chandelier of diamonds and having them valued at a couple of million dollars? Is that a trick question?"

Mary smiled. "Do you think Ernesto really thought it was fake?"

"That's what Ricardo told him to throw him off the scent. He wanted to earn something himself from his father's business. He's tired of being the sidekick and not getting anything out of it, not even any of the credit. Telling him it was fake served a purpose for Ernesto – it got him to the cash. And Ricardo would've got the diamonds if we hadn't found out what was going on. And if his father has been killed in that crash this morning he'll be too busy to worry about them until we're long gone."

"I'll be sorry to leave the ship. We made something of ourselves on there. Real careers."

"Yes but did you enjoy working inside all the time? Working every hour. What was it all for? Now we can enjoy life, visit some of those places we've been to before, but now actually see them for ourselves."

"I don't think so. I think we'll have to stay in Florida when we get there tomorrow. Maybe get different jobs, new identities. The money won't last forever. And he could come looking for us."

"We're not his first priority Mary. He will be looking for the person that killed his father, for the twenty million they stole. By the time he comes looking for us we will be long gone. There will be others looking to take over the business and he has to deal with them first, otherwise it will all collapse around him. Ricardo is ambitious, ruthless even, but he's not smart. He might not even last that long."

Chapter 17

Carlo felt like the third wheel sitting with Maria and Stephen. There was some kind of chemistry between them that made him feel like he shouldn't be there. He'd been around Maria a lot when she was with Ernesto, but she was always untouchable. Like royalty. He was there to serve, but not to interact. So as much as they had in common right now, they had come at it from very different angles. Even though she was no longer in the family, he felt a little awkward when they ran out of conversation.

He excused himself and left them to talk and decided to take a wander around the ship. He'd enjoyed the couple of days on board with his girlfriend, but he had really been working. She knew there was something going on but didn't ask too many questions. He had kept an eye on Barker on the ship, but they had spent a few hours on the beach in Bimini with most of the rest of the passengers and had spotted Maria. The new grey haircut was a dramatic change but he'd recognised her straight away. It would take more than a new hairstyle to hide from him.

He ventured up to the Lido Deck which was filling up with passengers settling in for the afternoon and looking forward to the early sail-away and to enjoying the ship while it was still quiet. After tomorrow in Florida it would be full to capacity and a lot more crowded and noisy. That was how it was meant to be.

Carlo hadn't had time to explore the ship in those two days so this was his opportunity, before they were certain Ricardo was on board, to get his bearings and understand how big a task it was going to be to spot someone and find them in such a big area. He didn't really know how well Lucy's plan was going to work but didn't have a better one himself. He was used to being given instructions, so planning ahead and working things out for himself were not usually required.

He walked through the Skyscape buffet and out to the aft of the ship, looking down onto another pool. Maybe he would be a passenger again soon if this worked out for him and he got out with some money and freedom. Not wanting to stay still for too long he headed back inside and down the aft stairs, through the casino, past lounges where musicians were preparing and bars being cleaned by the staff ready for the evening, always with one eye on access in and out, places where people could watch over each other, or hide from someone if necessary. The shops on Deck Five were impressive but closed right now until the ship sailed. They would no doubt be busy later.

The phone in his pocket suddenly rang. Ernesto's phone. It felt like a hot coal burning its way out of his jacket but he didn't want to touch it. It wouldn't stop ringing and he felt self-conscious ignoring it in front of all the passing strangers looking at him wondering when he was going to stop the ringing. He wandered towards the lifts and stepped inside one as it opened and pulled the phone out of his pocket. It was Ricardo.

Chapter 18

RICARDO

"*Carlo, it's me, Ricardo,*" he said, using his dead father's voice-mail inbox for the first time. "*I didn't expect you to pick up so I thought I'd leave you a little message. We saw you just now, on the Lido Deck, looking just like a tourist, enjoying life, waiting to go on holiday. I must say I was disappointed that we didn't find you in my father's Jaguar, alongside his burnt corpse. I assume that was Aidan, although I don't know why he would have been there instead of you. You failed my father Carlo. You failed in the biggest way possible. You know what that means.*"

I'll leave it there. You never get enough time in a voicemail to say what you really want to say, so that will have to do for now. But it's enough. It will serve its purpose: to make him scared, and to scare the others who are with him. It will sow doubt in their minds. Am I on the ship already? How could I possibly have got there? Did someone else see Carlo and report to me? Well, we'll let Carlo worry about that. He deserves it. They deserve it.

I threw up when I saw them bring my father out of that car. Anyone would be the same wouldn't they? It's not the sort of thing you want to see but I didn't just have to know whether he was dead. I had to know whether my time has come. Before now if I did the wrong thing my father would be the first to smack me down, to tell me I was wrong, to punish me for not doing it his way. But if he's gone I get to choose my own path, to decide what to do for myself. I feel sick and empty but I feel empowered and free now too.

Now I just have to work out how to get onto that ship.

Chapter 19

Starlight was ready to go back into regular service. There was a feeling all around the ship that things were back to normal, even on the quayside and in the town. The 'Ship of The Dead', as the local papers had called her, was yesterday's news. The authorities had done what they needed to do and the test cruise to Bimini had gone without a hitch, at least from the point of view of the crew and the ship itself. She was ready to sail with a full complement of passengers again, but that full complement was in Florida, and Starlight wasn't.

Originally, the plan had been to finish that test cruise in Fort Lauderdale, until they realised that the bulk of the passengers were locals from Nassau who, enticed by a cheap deal, wouldn't want to pay the extra cost of a flight home if they were dropped off in a different country. It would surely be better if they saved that money and spent it in the bars and casino. However, it was costing Galaxy Cruise Line a fortune to be docked for another day. A stationary ship bleeds money because its passengers are not spending on board and there are huge docking fees to account for. The only saving is on fuel.

But there was to be one more night of drama for Starlight. Had she been a person you might have warned her to prepare for it. As it was, nobody knew yet how it would take shape and who would come off worst, but there would certainly be more headlines, this time in the Fort Lauderdale newspapers.

A car with blacked-out windows drove slowly by the port gates, pausing briefly, then continued along the main road east. The face that was barely distinguishable through the darkened glass was that of Ricardo Gutierrez, surveying the scene and planning his day.

Chapter 20

Carlo looked unusually serious when he arrived back in the bar where he'd left Maria and Stephen. They'd finished their drinks and were about to look for Lucy or Barker to see if there was any news. "He's here. He's on the ship."

"What?" said Maria, "Who's here?"

"Ricardo. He rang me. Listen."

Carlo gave Maria Ernesto's phone and waited while she listened to the voicemail.

"Relax Carlo, he's probably just got the location of the phone after you turned the GPS back on, so he's calling it to spook us. You said yourself he would know we were on the ship. So it's no surprise really."

As Maria spoke, Ernesto's phone pinged. A text message arrived. There were no words, just an image. Maria's brow frowned as she squinted at the thumbnail image, tapped to enlarge it, and zoomed in. Then her face became more serious.

"It's you," she said, looking up at Carlo, "Here. On the ship."

Carlo grabbed the phone back and looked at the image. It was him on the Lido Deck about fifteen minutes ago. More sinister was the fact it was clearly taken by someone close by, not through a zoom lens from a hotel down-town, or from the top of another ship. This was taken by someone on board, someone nearby, someone who might have followed him or be watching them right now.

"He can't be here already Carlo, it's too soon," said Stephen, keen to keep a logical perspective, "But it does mean he has a contact on board. Maybe a new guest or, more likely, a crew member. Again though, that's not surprising."

"So what do we do about it?"

"Well we wanted to lure him on board, so it's working right?" said Maria, "Maybe we have to put Lucy's plan into action sooner and start watching out for each other. That way if anything happens to one of us at least someone else will know about it and be able to help or tell the others."

"When do we sail?"

"Two O'clock I think."

"So we have a couple of hours to find this person?"

"Find him?"

"Yes. Barker is watching the doors for people coming on board. You should go and help him because you know Ricardo and some of his men. They don't know you Stephen so you should come with me while I walk around the ship again and watch out for anyone who might be following me. They won't notice you if you are careful. You can do that?"

Stephen nodded, looked at Maria, and back to Carlo, "Let's go."

Chapter 21

Lucy walked quickly when she left the office where Barker was examining the video feed from the gangway. She suddenly felt very vulnerable being on her own, a feeling she'd never felt before on the ship despite all that had happened in previous weeks. This time the threat was very real and very final, and she felt bad leaving Barker in the office on his own. There would be other crew members wandering in and out but they didn't know the danger he could be in. She thought he would feel better with people around him, and for the same reason she tried to stick to the busy areas of the ship rather than taking shortcuts down corridors where escape was impossible.

Mark and Sam, the guitarists from her band, were setting up their equipment in the Explorers Lounge when she walked in. "Morning you two," she said as brightly as she could manage under the circumstances.

"Ah, Lucy," said Mark, "We were just getting worried you might not show. It's not like you to be late."

"No, not normally. But I've got bad news. I've spent all morning in the bathroom throwing up. Must've eaten something bad last night. I daren't risk performing until later today, maybe this evening if I feel better."

"Oh no, that is bad. Philipe said the same yesterday, that's why he's late, but he'll be OK later. Must be something going around. We'd better get one of the theatre team to stand in for you. We'll manage, but only for a day. You'd better be OK tomorrow, you're the headline act," Mark smiled at Lucy.

"Thanks Mark. I'm really sorry. Where are you going to be playing most of the day?" Lucy was keen to avoid being seen wandering round looking like she was enjoying herself when she was supposed to be sick.

"In here and the Atrium I think. The Lido Deck is covered by the DJ this afternoon and evening, so it's not as busy as usual with half the guests not here. Once we get to Florida though it'll be back to business as usual."

"Yeah, I'm looking forward to it – a bit of normality," Lucy rolled her eyes and smiled. "I'll see you all later." As she walked out of the bar she bumped into Philipe on his way in and explained the situation again, then headed back towards the bar where she'd last seen Maria and Stephen.

Chapter 22

The door nearest Barker's desk clicked open unusually slowly, enough to make him nervous. Normally it was a crew member rushing in and out in a hurry and then letting the damn thing slam on the way out. This time though it was a familiar face that peered around. Maria.

She stepped inside the office, nodding towards the only other person at a desk at the back of the room as if to ask Barker if it was OK that she came in. Barker gestured towards a spare swivel chair at the desk behind him and Maria pulled it around and sat down. Given that she was dressed unusually low-key for her, she would not be noticed too much if she sat with him and looked like she was busy.

"Any news?" she said quietly.

"Nothing. But then I don't really know who I'm looking for. It's hard to work from a quick look at a phone photo."

"You'd know him if you saw him. Ricardo doesn't do disguise. He's too arrogant for that. He normally wants to be recognised."

"But maybe not today?"

"Maybe not."

"He must know that we're waiting for him?"

"Oh, I don't know. You forget he doesn't live in the real

world. He's only ever known life as a prince, an heir to a dynasty. Everything laid on a plate for him. He thinks Ernesto was hard on him, but that's only like any parent giving their kids boundaries. Ricardo's boundaries were a lot broader than most people's, so anyone telling him not to do something or preventing him, soon became a problem."

"How did you cope with him?"

"Charm. He's a creep. If I fluttered my eyelashes he would back down. He couldn't help himself. I'm not kidding myself though. I know he doesn't like me, so I'm not going to be able to talk him out of anything I'm afraid."

"How do you think he's going to play this today? Turn up himself or send his goons?"

"Both, maybe? He's not capable of taking us on by himself I don't think, plus he'll want to be here to bask in the glory and take the credit if he succeeds."

"And will he? Succeed I mean?"

"I hope not. For all our sakes. We have the numbers, but he's a sneaky little shit." Maria's eyes widened and she pointed at the monitor, "Our friends are back."

Barker squinted at the image of two people coming through the scanners at the gangway entrance. Jose Ramirez and Mary Tkachuk having their passes scanned. "Who's side are they on?"

"Oh, they helped Ernesto from time to time, but they're only in it for themselves, trust me."

"They're not alone," said Barker fixing Maria with a hard stare.

Maria paused and then smiled gently, realising what she'd walked into, "OK, yes, you're right, me too. Is that what you want me to say?"

"You betrayed me."

"I used you to get at the money John, but I didn't hurt you."

"You hurt Lucy."

"Yes...I did. But I was mad, I was running away and I wasn't aiming at her, just at the group."

"So you could've hit me?"

"I didn't think I'd hit anybody. I was on a lifeboat bobbing on the sea waving a tiny pistol at a hole in the side of the ship." Maria stopped and shook her head. "I'm sorry. I know you think I'm a bad person but the stuff I told you about my background is all true. About my children, about Michael and Vega. I got him back for coming for me and my children. The money? That just appeared in front of us. Neither of us expected that."

"You came after it again last week, then took me to Gutierrez, to Ernesto, when I didn't give it to you."

"When I leave here tomorrow John, I go back to my old life. I have no job, no income, no sugar daddy any more. I have to look after my daughter, protect her. A parent has to find a way. That was my chance. I thought it would be easy but I was wrong. Can we get past this? For twenty-four hours? Then you never have to see me again."

Barker shrugged.

"You are lucky, John. You have Lucy. You're getting the best deal out of all of this, something more important than money. In another lifetime I should have looked for a man like you. But there aren't many of them where I come from. Too much poverty, too much crime. You are from the other side. We are very different, but I wish I was more like you."

Chapter 23

Lucy walked into the Atrium and looked over the balcony at the passengers coming back on board. It wasn't as busy as it normally would be but she should be entertaining them today as they arrived and then again in the evening. She felt bad for letting the boys in the band down but didn't really have a choice. She felt sure they would understand if they knew the truth. Maybe one day she could tell them.

Suddenly she stepped back from the railing as she recognised Mary Tkachuk walking across the dance floor below. She assumed Barker would have seen her on the cameras as well, and wondered if Ramirez had been with her. Mary would be used to seeing Lucy around the ship under normal circumstances, but maybe not today, this particular morning. She would know what had happened earlier, but not what they had done next or what they were planning to do about it. She had seemingly been loyal to Ernesto up until then, but what about Ricardo? Was she being used by him? Lucy couldn't be sure why but her instinct told her that wasn't the case. Mary was younger than Ernesto but older and more mature than Ricardo and had worked her way up the ladder in her career. She couldn't imagine her being bullied by a twenty-something wannabe gangster. Maybe she should take a leaf out of her book.

Lucy could see that the table where they'd all sat in the bar on the other side of the Atrium was now empty, so the others must've dispersed. She felt alone and vulnerable again and looked around like a startled rabbit. Then she noticed Maria on the opposite side of the Atrium on the same deck, looking across at her, nodding once. Was this how the day was going to be? This was her plan: to move around the ship and look out for suspicious activity, while knowing that someone else was looking out for her. She felt a sudden rush of confidence as she realised she was well-placed to spot the odd one out in a bunch of tourists. She knew what the typical behaviour of a cruise ship passenger was likely to be: relaxed, happy, chilled, holding a drink in their hand, or sitting with one at a table somewhere. She would surely spot someone looking tense, with a serious expression looking out for her or Barker or Stephen. But who would they come for first? How would they approach the task of harming them if they stayed in public places? Laura had managed it before though, hadn't she? But then she'd had the element of surprise, nobody was expecting that. This time they would be ready for the killer and have the upper hand.

Lucy's phone pinged in her pocket, a message from Maria:

We should eat. Follow me to Skyscape restaurant. Sit at different tables but facing so we can see each other?

Lucy didn't reply but just looked up at Maria who saw her and headed for the staircase. They had made the decision not to use the lifts in case a random stranger stepped into one with them. At the very least it would be unsettling. At worst it could be fatal.

She began to think back to this morning when all she and Barker had to do was escape from Ernesto Gutierrez and how that had resolved itself, albeit more by luck than judgement.

Instead, she now had a life-or-death situation to deal with that apparently had a fixed timeline. Ricardo couldn't follow them onto American soil and risk getting caught out there. He'd have to finish the job on board and then find a way of leaving without being caught. She shuddered as it dawned on her...so would they.

Chapter 24

I hate the waiting, thought Stephen, as he wandered outside along Deck Seventeen, a discrete distance behind Carlo, who suddenly stopped and leaned over the railing to take a look at what was happening on the Lido deck below. Stephen turned right, following the railing around to the opposite side of the ship where he and Carlo could keep an eye out for each other whilst also surveying the decks and scanning for unusual activity. It occurred to him that neither he nor Carlo were regular cruisers so were unlikely to spot anything out of the ordinary in that respect, but he was reassured that Carlo knew the Gutierrez family and most of the people who worked for them, so was possibly the best spotter of trouble.

Stephen also felt safer than he imagined the others would because Ricardo had no idea who he was or what he looked like, so was unlikely to come for him first. Did that put an extra burden of responsibility on him to protect Carlo or whoever else he would be paired up with today because he might go unnoticed? Maybe, but he felt confident he was in a good position to do so.

In the Seascape restaurant, one deck below Lucy and Maria sat at separate tables about eight rows apart, facing one another. Maria had quickly grabbed a plate on the way in and picked up some fish and rice and some cutlery before finding her table. Lucy took that to mean she could take a little more time as Maria would be watching out for her while she chose something to eat, providing she stayed within sight. But she didn't feel particularly hungry. Ten days ago the woman now looking out for her safety had shot her in the leg. Why was she suddenly the one to trust with her life? Because she was a part of the world that was coming after them and knew how it worked. It was actually her that had killed Ernesto this morning, even if it was unintentional. No-one else, not even Carlo, was particularly upset for Ernesto. But it wasn't just Maria that Ricardo was coming for was it? They were all in his sights, so it was probably best to all stick together and look after each other...for now.

Lucy grabbed a coffee and some salad, cheese, and cooked meats and sat down to eat, glancing in the direction of Maria to check where she was, but not straight at her, so nobody watching would know they were connected in any way. She looked out of the window onto the quayside where the queue of passengers embarking was dwindling down to a trickle. It wouldn't be long before the gangway was closed and the captain made preparations to leave. That's when the problems would really begin.

Chapter 25

A mile away from the cruise port a black Range Rover swept around the roundabout in front of a luxury hotel and pulled up outside the front door. The hotel doorman obviously recognised the vehicle because instead of approaching to open the back door he stepped back and deferred to the sharp-suited men who stepped out of the front, one walking up the steps to open the door of the hotel, and the other opening the car door itself for the important occupant to step out.

A young man appeared from inside the car, wearing a tailor-made suit with expensive, highly polished shoes and mirrored silver sunglasses. He was of average height and build and resembled Ramirez from Starlight but for the fifteen-year age difference, a visibly easier upbringing, and more expensive haircut, which he immediately covered with a brand new designer baseball cap. All three men walked up the steps and into the building, straight into the restaurant to the usual table on the terrace which was suitably private. Two of the men stepped back and allowed the head waiter to seat the VIP and ask if he would like his usual choice. The VIP agreed and the waiter scuttled away, instructing the sommelier to take a bottle of Dom Perignon to Mr Gutierrez.

But this wasn't Mr Gutierrez, it was his body double. The

real Ricardo Gutierrez was, at the same time, stepping out of the back of a taxi by the cruise port gates wearing substantially cheaper sunglasses and a scruffy baseball cap, with ripped jeans and a Hard Rock Cafe T-shirt a couple of sizes too big hanging off his shoulders. He picked up a small rucksack and slung it over his shoulder, handed some cash to the driver and closed the door behind him. Then he walked through the gates, not straight towards Starlight, but past the first building where Lucy had met Ashton, which now had new windows and frames painted to hide the bullet marks from that eventful evening, and turned left towards a smaller building where he disappeared inside.

In the office on board Starlight Barker was struggling to keep his eyes and his mind focussed on the screen showing the feed from the gangway. The numbers embarking had dropped off completely now, with only one or two boarding every minute. He jumped when the phone rang and Dennis, one of the crew who had called into the office before swapping shifts to take over at the door, confirmed that everyone was accounted for, as he'd requested. Once that news was relayed upstairs to the bridge it would not be long before they got underway.

Lucy opened the door and stepped in with a cup of coffee for Barker to top up his caffeine levels, "Maria's outside. I should get back. We said we wouldn't be out of sight of each other for more than a couple of minutes."

"How's that going?"

"Fine. We don't have to speak to each other except for the odd message. I think we would run out of conversation pretty quickly. 'So, how's the bullet wound I gave ya?'" Lucy smiled. "Maybe you should hang out with her instead if you like? I'm

73

sure you two will get along. Like you did before."

"Actually I'm done here so I might join you both."

"Already? That's early."

"The ship's less than half full so she'll be ready to go soon. I think we'll leave early. Where are Stephen and Carlo?"

"On deck, I think. All they need to do for now is keep an eye out for each other."

"We can't just sit and wait for something to happen though, we've got to be proactive."

"I thought you weren't keen on doing this?"

"I'm not, but if we have to be here in this situation I'd rather be in control of it than let some scumbag decide our fate. We need to work out how best to lure him out."

"We don't even know that he's on board yet do we? Any sign of him?"

"No sign. But my gut feeling tells me he'll be here."

"Yes...I feel the same. I've never met him but I can feel that he's here. Or is that just fear?"

"Well, it's time to find out. Maria is the expert manipulator. We'll go and see what she thinks we can do to make him show his face."

Chapter 26

Once the lines were released from the quayside, Captain Trulli began to manoeuvre Starlight out from her berth and head out of the port and into open water. At the same time, a tiny pilot boat followed at a safe distance behind in order to collect the man on the bridge helping Trulli to navigate the tight confines of the cruise port and put the ship on a safe course out to sea.

The atmosphere on the bridge was serious but relaxed. The crew members were happy to be taking Starlight back into regular service and a routine they were used to again. When the ship was safely on course the captain wished the pilot well and shook his hand before relieving him of his duties and dismissing him. The pilot, a local man called Denzel who had worked in the port for nearly thirty years, exited the bridge and headed downstairs. As he did so the bridge radioed to the pilot boat that he was on his way, so it could manoeuvre into position next to the gangway exit on the port side of the ship where it would steady itself enough to allow Denzel to hop back on board and take him home.

Five minutes later the portly figure of a middle-aged man resembling Denzel appeared at the doorway, turned his back to the ocean, and gripped the ladder he would have to climb down to get to the level of the pilot boat. It was a task he'd performed thousands of times, getting off a big ship when it left, and getting on them when they arrived in port. Denzel knew that this was the only really difficult and dangerous part of his job. His experience of sailing in and out of Nassau was vast, so that came naturally to him and was enjoyable. But hopping off a 150,000-tonne ship onto a tiny motor boat bobbing around in its wake was always going to be a risk, especially now arthritis was making itself felt in his knees. One slip and he'd be in the ocean, bobbing around between the two vessels, just a few seconds bad luck away from being crushed between them. Sooner or later he would have to retire. His wife would kill him if he died while at work.

With a neat little step whilst looking intently at the pilot boat's deck movements, Denzel hopped back on board and was grabbed tightly by a fellow crew member and helped into the small interior where his deputy was at the helm. Usually, the boat would immediately peel away out of the danger of the wash of such a huge ship, but this time wasn't usual. A small, wiry man in his late twenties wearing overalls, a baseball cap and life jacket did the reverse of Denzel's procedure. The man on the pilot boat deck helped guide him to the edge of the boat next to Starlight and shouted, "Now!" when it was safe to grab the ladder. As soon as the man was detached from the pilot boat and started climbing the ladder on Starlight's side, it pulled away, turned, and headed back to the port. The man carefully climbed the last half-dozen rungs of the ladder and was helped on board by the crew members, disappearing inside the ship as the door was closed behind him.

Chapter 27

RICARDO

That was cool. If I had to have a normal job I'd do something on the sea. And the pilot is the main man in any port. He knows everything about the place. That's why my father got to know him twenty years ago. That's how we bring things in and out when we need to without much hassle. It was scary too though. I don't know how that old man jumps on and off that little boat bouncing around next to a hulk of a ship like that. One slip and you're gone, man. He's got some balls.

Now to the business at hand, get changed and blend in and feel my way around, see what I can see. But they will be looking for me. They might even have seen me from the upper decks when I jumped on board, but I doubt it. They're not that smart. How many people bother to watch the pilot jumping on and off, and yet it's a dramatic event happening right under their noses? I don't care if they did see. I will disappear into the depths of the ship and they will have no clue where I am or where I'm coming from. Or when.

I need to be careful though. There are five of them and one of me, although there is help on board for me if I need it. But it's best if I do this myself, that way there's less to go wrong and I'm in control. Also, I get the pleasure of avenging my father and settling some scores. I don't know for sure which one of them killed him, but I know who didn't. It wasn't the cop or his girlfriend because that's who my father was following. They were in the SUV, about to load it with the cash they stole. They would've had the opportunity when they got cornered but my father was burned in his car when it was hit by another. I don't think they could've done that. But they stole millions from him that they think is theirs, which put him in that place at that time and led to his death. So they have to go too.

Carlo was with him. He must've betrayed him because if he hadn't he would've died too. And the other body in the car wasn't him. It was the girl's father. Last time I saw him was when we put him in the boot of the SUV. So someone, probably Carlo, has moved him. He would have to do that to try to cover his tracks. He forgot I have friends in the mortuary. I cannot allow him to live after doing that. Both of us will not leave this ship alive.

Then there's Maria. The witch that snubbed me because I wasn't important enough and blatantly slept with my father just to get at his money and his lifestyle. But maybe I've had some of that myself. It comes with the territory. Greedy girls are not hard to come by when they see what a life they could have with a family like ours. It was her that rented the other car. There's footage of her picking it up. That was careless of her. She thinks she's smart but she's an amateur. Maybe she drove into the back of the Jaguar on the spur of the moment to make some sort of statement. It might even have been accidental but it doesn't make any difference. She caused my father's death one way or the other.

When I'm done I will get off the ship the way I got on, then sneak on a ferry back home. They are all taking their last journey tonight.

Chapter 28

Mary Tkachuk let herself into her staff cabin. It was tiny, just big enough for a single bed, a dresser with a half-length mirror, and a small shower room with toilet and sink. She was lucky to have a room of her own, unlike most of the people that worked under her who would share with at least one other person. Her relationship with Ramirez was not public. Most people knew something was going on but neither talked about it to anyone else and they spent almost no time together outside of work, if only so they had the option of not being linked to each other when it came to their side hustles.

When she rang Ramirez Mary could hear engine room noise in the background so had to raise her voice. "She's back," she shouted, "The singer. I saw her in the Atrium after we got back on board."

"So? She works here Mary," said Ramirez in reply.

"I know, but I thought...I thought after what happened...what might've happened this morning, she might be...they might not make it back."

"We don't know what happened. I said we should've stuck around to find out but you wanted to get out of there fast so we just ran." Ramirez looked around him to see if anyone was listening in. There were a couple of other engineers in sight but they were out of hearing range. He'd slid one side of his ear defenders up over his head so he could listen to her.

"They weren't supposed to come back here. I thought Ernesto and Carlo would get the money and get rid of them. Or *they* would get the money and get away from Ernesto and disappear."

"Well Ernesto wasn't in a good way when we ran, was he? Maybe Carlo got the money instead."

"Will this affect our deal?"

"I don't see how. We have what we need. The deal is on for tonight. I've had a text from them to say the product is here. We pay them in a few hours and meet our buyer in the morning when we dock. This time tomorrow we'll be very wealthy people."

"What about Ricardo?"

"What about him? Whatever has happened to Ernesto means Ricardo will be occupied. If he's alive he will be telling Ricardo all about it and if he's dead, Ricardo will be furious. Either way, he'll be going after whoever was driving that car. And it wasn't the girl or the cop. There's no reason why we should worry about him."

Chapter 29

Ernesto's phone buzzed gently in Carlo's pocket, making him jump. Maria smiled gently at her mischievousness – she could have texted him on his own mobile but thought this would get his attention quicker.

I need Ricardo's number. I deleted him, can you find it on there and send it to me?

Carlo's heart rate slowed down with relief as he cursed Maria, then swiped through the contacts to find the number and reply to her.

What are you going to do with it?

You'll see. Stay there and keep an eye on the pools.

Carlo was puzzled but texted the number back and waited, checking that Stephen was still within sight on the other side of the deck. He had moved to a seat at a table close enough to the bar to blend in, but near enough to the railings overlooking the Lido deck below that he could still see half of the area. He expected that Carlo would eventually move around to cover the other half.

The pool was filling up slowly and the loungers surrounding it were gaining more sunbathers applying sunscreen and reading books and magazines in the warm afternoon sun. Carlo remembered that for everyone else on the ship, this was a happy occasion and he should try not to look too serious or out of place. In his trademark black jeans and tailored white shirt, he didn't look like a sun worshipper, or particularly like a holidaymaker, which meant moving around from time to time to avoid catching the eye of anyone for too long that they would wonder what he was up to. A lot of the other passengers were toing and froing so nobody would notice another stranger moving around the decks.

What quite a few of them did notice was the tall, slim, olive-skinned woman in a yellow swimsuit putting a bag down on a vacant sun-lounger, arranging a fresh towel over the top of it and walking over to the shower at one end of the pool, rinsing herself off and then lowering herself down the metal ladder into the heated pool. Carlo was sure he detected a lowering of the background noise on the Lido deck as people stopped talking.

It had been Lucy's idea. Remembering how Maria had distracted Barker when they first met in the same place a couple of weeks ago she asked Maria if she still had the distinctive costume in her suitcase. This time with short, cropped grey hair instead of the long dark hair Barker remembered, she was just as noticeable on board a typical cruise ship full of middle-aged travellers used to over-indulging on free food and expensive drinks packages. At just turned forty years old, nearly six feet tall barefoot, slim but with appropriate curves, Maria stood out like a sore thumb, particularly with that acid yellow swimsuit against her olive skin. Lucy felt the need to remind Barker that this was work not pleasure, and that they should be watching everywhere *but* Maria, looking out for reactions on the faces of onlookers who might want to report this sighting to a certain recently-promoted drug boss.

It had been Maria's idea to up the ante and send a photo of

herself in her room wearing the swimsuit to Ricardo. *What the hell,* she thought, *he knows we're here, we know he's here. So let's stop messing around and make the first move. Maybe I can make him drop his guard.*

The chins of several male and female sunbathers dropped as she came back out of the pool, hair immaculately dry having not been anywhere near the water, and swung around to sit on the edge with her lower legs dangling in the water, pretending not to notice the attention she was receiving, whilst hoping that either Ricardo or one of his informants would walk by and react or report.

Maria felt safe in the knowledge that Barker and Lucy had preceded her onto the Lido deck and positioned themselves port and starboard at tables under the shelter of the deck above with a view of the pool, hoping to be able to notice people's reactions and movements. Also, she knew that Carlo and Stephen were watching from above. How long could she reasonably sit there posing for Ricardo and friends? Half an hour maybe? If he had any contacts anywhere on that deck they would surely notice in that time, and if not word would spread fast enough. She could always slip back into the pool again looking like she needed to cool off or go back to her lounger and apply some sunscreen, since the weather was getting warmer. Much like the atmosphere around the pool.

Chapter 30

Twelve decks below the Lido Deck a pallet was being pushed on a trolley down a long crew-only corridor from the midships cargo door towards the aft end of the ship. On the pallet was a shrink-wrapped crate loaded onto the ship only a couple of hours ago, containing what appeared to be plumbing spares: pipes and joints and adaptors of various sizes, packed with paper and polystyrene chips and sealed carefully into place. Artur, the man pushing the trolley, stopped at a large lift and pressed the down arrow call button on the wall next to it. Twenty seconds later the lift doors opened and he pushed the trolley inside. The word SPARES was printed in black letters on a white A4 sticker on the top of the black shrink wrap. Artur pressed the button that said *Engineering*, watched the doors close, and stared around the stainless steel cube like every other solo lift passenger wasting time for the few seconds it took to get from A to B. He didn't care what was in the pallet. It was just his job to deliver it.

The lift stopped and the doors opened and Artur looked out onto a busy corridor full of people in dirty overalls walking right-to-left and left-to-right looking like they were all extremely busy. He pushed the pallet out tentatively not wanting to cause injury or delay anybody, and looked from side to side to find a gap in the human traffic. He had to hold the lift doors open a couple of times while he waited and then pushed hard. The trolley clunked over the edge of the lift floor and out into the corridor, swinging round to the left as Artur guided it like a huge, wayward shopping trolley towards the engineering store room, which was only a few metres away but around the corner of the corridor facing the aft of the ship with a view of the churning wake, so he had to shift its weight and slide it out, temporarily blocking the way for most of the technicians trying to get past, and then pushed it along and around before stopping in front of the large metal door to the store room.

Luckily for Artur someone was coming out of the room and opened the door for him, pointing out a space on the right-hand side where the pallet could be left. The man casually checked the paperwork, then left Artur to finish the move. He dropped the pallet down on the floor and pulled the trolley out from under it, then began the reverse procedure of taking the trolley back up to the cargo door for loading or unloading in Florida tomorrow. As he walked his mind drifted to what might be on offer in the staff canteen this afternoon as he was already late for his lunch and that was his next stop.

Chapter 31

Barker soon saw the flaw in the plan. The idea was to get Ricardo's attention, either directly or indirectly through someone working on board who might be getting paid to pass on information. But as he sat watching the bar tenders' heads swivel as they walked by and bumped into furniture, he wondered how, if *everybody* was looking at Maria, he would pick out anyone suspiciously doing so, unless Ricardo himself showed up, which was unlikely. And what would they do if he did?

He messaged Lucy across the other side of the deck just out of sight.

Just thinking that myself, she replied. *Let her have her moment in the sun and soak up the attention. At least the word will get to you-know-who.*

On the deck above Stephen smiled at Maria's audacity and, to an extent, bravery. Ricardo would be very stupid to try anything out there in full view, but she was deliberately winding up a dangerous man who she knew didn't like her very much and had a very big score to settle. He also couldn't help but wonder what would happen if circumstances were different and they got to know each other better. Maybe tomorrow he could begin to find out if he made the extra effort to make sure she stayed alive until then.

Carlo, standing by the railing casually looking at his phone, was shaking his head at the swimsuit photo Maria had also sent to him as well as Ricardo. He knew Ricardo well enough to know how that would make him react and wondered if it was absolutely necessary. But then what else were they supposed to do? They were here to find him and deal with him and couldn't just sit waiting for something to happen. But this might not be the right place to expect him to break cover. Ricardo was a fool, but not completely stupid.

A bartender pushing a trolley full of drinks in a large tub of ice approached along the deck between two rows of sun-loungers and held a bottle out in front of Carlo.

"Cold beer sir?"

Carlo hadn't eaten or drunk anything for a couple of hours and the weather was warming up on the top deck, so he decided that one drink wouldn't do any harm. It was just weak yellow fizz anyway and wouldn't cloud his judgment but the ice it had been sat in would cool him down. He reached out to take the beer from the man's hand as the waiter grabbed his bottle opener. Just as he was about to open it Carlo thought better of it and selected another bottle from the other end of the cart, smiling at the waiter. "I prefer this one," he said as he looked him in the eye to try to detect a giveaway expression of disappointment. Maybe he was overreacting but it did no harm to be careful.

Chapter 32

Ramirez was in the queue at the buffet in the crew mess, hoping for his first proper meal of the day. He filled his plate with chicken and rice and beans and grabbed a coffee on his way to a table in the furthest corner where he had arranged to meet Mary Tkachuk. She was already there, tucking into steak and eggs and sipping iced water. Neither being the type to show much emotion, they just nodded at each other in acknowledgment at first as they were both hungry and keen to get some food down them. They usually took their breaks at odd times when the canteen was quieter, mainly so they could speak more privately.

"Heard anything?" Mary said.

Ramirez nodded and gave her a look that said, *Yes, but don't ask me to say it out loud in here.*

"When?" Mary persisted.

"Don't know yet," Ramirez said after swallowing the first big mouthful of chicken, "They will let us know at the last minute. This afternoon most probably."

"Do we know them?"

"We know who they work for, but not who is doing the trade. They will just be some chancers doing it for a cut, a bit like us I guess. The main man isn't going to come and supervise. They will be somebody expendable just in case, so that the boss stays

88

clean and can deny everything."

"I'm nervous, but at least now there's a good chance Ernesto will never find out we're buying stuff from his competition."

"See? I told you it would be OK. No need to worry about it. We switched allegiance at just the right time."

"How does it work?"

"They tell us where the goods are. We check it's what we ordered and hand over the payment. Then we split it down and pack it as we discussed and take it out to hand over to the buyer at the port and walk away with two million in cash and disappear."

"Won't they look for us when we don't come back?"

"I've already sorted that. My cousin will scan our cards back in so they'll sail without us, thinking we're on board but they just won't be able to find us straight away."

"Is that safe?"

"Yes. I just told him we wanted a few extra hours ashore. He won't care. He's done it himself before."

"Where do we go after that?"

"Anywhere we like. It's best that we don't make any plans: if we don't know where we're going yet nobody else can predict it can they?" Ramirez cracked a rare smile to reassure Mary, who wasn't quite so sure.

Chapter 33

Maria had been sitting by the pool for fifteen minutes when a noise behind her stood out from the background buzz of the Lido Deck. It was her mobile phone ringing in the bag she'd put on the sun lounger. She had no idea who could be ringing her right now. The others watching her had agreed they would only use messages and nobody else knew where she was. Except...

Ignoring the ringing phone Maria slipped back into the pool for a couple of minutes before climbing out and showering again, lowering the volume on deck once more. She stepped carefully across to her sun lounger and picked up the fresh towel and wrapped it around her, again pretending to be oblivious to the attention she was receiving. She sat back and reached into her bag for a paperback and casually picked her phone out at the same time, looking at the home screen for an indication of who had rung her.

She recognised the number immediately. Ricardo. He had seldom rung her in the past but each time he had she'd squirmed and usually ignored it, with the attitude of, *If it's important, Ernesto will tell me*. With him gone she wanted to ignore it but knew that she couldn't. A notification told of the missed call but the one that mattered was the text message. She opened it up tentatively and saw that it was just a photo. A photo taken in a cabin like hers. The image showed a short, blue, body-hugging dress laid out on the bed accompanied by two words: *my favourite.*

Maria's stomach flipped over, "What a creep," she muttered almost loudly enough for people nearby to hear, whilst trying to appear calm and not as freaked out as she was feeling. So that she could feel in control of the situation she immediately forwarded the image to the others, including the words 'He's definitely here.'

Copying everyone in to her reply, Lucy sent a message back: *Uurgh. I didn't like the sound of him before. Now I like him even less. You can't go back to your cabin.*

Maria replied with: *No, I don't think any of us can. But I have no other clothes.*

After a few seconds Lucy replied, '*Not a problem. Wardrobe will sort you out in the theatre. Meet me in the Ladies' toilets in fifteen minutes. Gents, will one of you sit within sight of the door and keep your eyes open for undesirables please?*'

Barker replied, *On my way* and found an empty seat at a table in a corner of the pool deck about thirty feet away from the ladies' toilets. He sat with his back to the windows on the starboard side that looked out onto the ocean and instead faced the throng of passengers enjoying themselves around the pool. He ignored Maria as she walked past five minutes later carrying the drink she'd been sipping by the pool. Maria ignored him in return and walked casually through the door into the safety of the ladies' room.

Barker opened the notepad he'd brought with him from the office and started scribbling nonsense on a random page in the middle so it looked like he was doing something other than sitting by the pool passing the time of day. He was well aware that he should be doing something constructive that he could demonstrate to the captain about his new role, which in fact he was. Finding a career criminal who has boarded the ship in order to murder several of its passengers is about the most constructive security job you can have. But that didn't stop him from feeling bad because he'd enticed this particular career criminal on board in the first place. At least he knew who the only people at risk were likely to be and no innocent holidaymakers were in danger. Probably.

A couple of minutes later Lucy also ignored Barker as she walked past and pushed open the door to the ladies' toilets and went inside. He took the opportunity to relax a little and look around now that he knew Maria and Lucy were together. Nobody else had entered or left. Life on the ship was getting busy with people wandering back and forth between the pool and the buffet, the Lido Deck and the deck above which was better for sunbathing. Some people waved at passing waiters to get their drinks, others wandered to the bar to get their own. All very normal, he decided, with his growing knowledge of passenger life on a cruise ship. He couldn't make out any odd or unusual behaviour, which was a speciality of his from his time as a police officer, watching scenes unfold and spotting what looked out of place.

"John! Come with me," Lucy shook him out of his daydream.

"What? Where?"

"In here," said Lucy, grabbing him by the hand and pulling him up out of his seat.

"I can't go in there," Barker started to resist but Lucy yanked his arm harder and they both crashed through the door to the ladies' bathroom.

"In there," Lucy pointed at the middle of three cubicles.

"Look underneath."

Barker could see by the expression on her face that she was deadly serious. He crouched down and put his hands on the floor and turned his head to look under the middle cubicle door, while Lucy backed up against the entrance to prevent anyone else from coming in. Slumped in a heap on the floor in the cubicle was a woman in a yellow swimsuit, face down on the cold tiles. He could see the right side of her face, and noticed her right eye open and glazed.

Lucy was beginning to get too used to these types of situations and knew that the seriousness of the circumstances is often confirmed by a random thought passing through your mind. On this occasion it was that for this beautiful, poised, elegant woman to find herself in a horrible mess on the floor of a toilet, something terrible had to have happened. But Maria had only been in there a few minutes so there might be some hope.

"Get help," Barker said to Lucy.

"I can't leave. People will see."

"Just stand on the other side of the door and grab the first person in a uniform and bring them inside. If anyone tries to get in tell them someone has passed out and you're waiting for first aid."

Barker turned and pushed open the door of the adjacent cubicle, put down the lid of the toilet and stood on it. He pulled on the partition to see if it would take his weight and hoisted himself up onto the top of it on his waist, trying to swing his right leg up to climb over, but thought better of it and reached his arm down towards the lock on the cubicle door. With some precarious balancing and a scary moment when he thought he was going to fall over and land on Maria, he pushed back the lock on the door and dropped back down into his own cubicle.

The entrance door burst open and Lucy dragged in a bartender who looked terrified at being pulled into the ladies' toilets by a mad woman. As he looked up at Barker pushing the door of the middle cubicle open to reveal Maria's lifeless body, he looked even more serious but knew what to do, "I'll call the doctor."

"I don't think the doctor can help now," Barker said as he put his hand on Maria's shoulder and tried to rouse her, "I'll have to give it a go."

"Don't wait John, they could be ages," said Lucy. "There are hardly any medical staff and it could take them ten minutes to get here."

Barker hooked his hands under Maria's armpits pulling her twisted body out of the cubicle and turned her onto her back. His first aid training hadn't been tested in a few years but the basics were simple: if there's no response and you're not in danger, go straight to CPR.

Lucy saw the irony of Barker giving mouth-to-mouth to a woman he'd admired, hated and was now collaborating with. She had even almost killed her. But right now *she* was the victim and he was going to be professional and give her a fighting chance. Maria lay there lifeless in nothing but that yellow swimsuit on the cold hard floor, all of her impressive dignity disappearing along with her chances of survival.

Lucy watched as Barker knelt down next to Maria, leaned over, took hold of her mouth and jaw and breathed deeply into her lungs several times. He then sat up and placed the heels of both hands between her breasts and pushed sharply down on her chest a dozen times in an attempt to restart her heart. He alternated between the two for five minutes, had a few seconds rest, and then continued.

Eventually, Lucy offered to take over from Barker, but he

seemed intent on continuing by himself. She couldn't see where he was getting the energy from but was relieved as it had been years since her last first aid course and she had never actually done it for real.

The door burst open again, this time for three people: a woman in a white medical uniform carrying a bag of equipment and two men carrying a folding stretcher.

"Anything?" said the doctor. Barker shook his head. "Thank you. We'll take over now. Wait outside for us please."

Barker and Lucy got to their feet and stumbled out through the door, turning back to see the doctor start to examine Maria. Outside, a couple of office staff guarded the door and smiled sympathetically as they sat down at the table Barker had been sitting at earlier. A couple of minutes later the toilet door opened and the two men came out carrying Maria on the stretcher with a blanket over her body including her face. The doctor followed but didn't acknowledge them, instead skipping past the stretcher so she could call for the nearest lift to take Maria down to the medical centre.

Chapter 34

"What the hell happened?!" said Carlo when he and Stephen joined Barker and Lucy on the sun deck overlooking the bow of the ship as it continued northwest away from Nassau and towards Florida. Being exposed to the wind, the area was less popular with sunbathers so the group could gather to talk without being overheard, and also see people coming from all directions.

"I followed her in and found her on the floor in a cubicle," replied Lucy.

"But you said there was nobody else in there."

"There wasn't."

"And nobody went in or out?" said Carlo looking at Barker for confirmation. Barker just shook his head.

"How is that possible? She walks in perfectly fine, then dies on the fricking toilet."

"She wasn't on the toilet."

"You said she was in a cubicle."

"Yes, but she...she was on the floor. She wasn't...using the toilet. The towel she had wrapped round her when she went in looked like it came off when she fell on the floor. I think she was just sitting on the toilet waiting for me to arrive. Otherwise, she would've felt weird if someone else came in and she was just standing there doing nothing."

"You hated her Lucy. She shot you two weeks ago and this was your chance to get her back for that."

"What?!"

"Hold on," said Barker, "Lucy wouldn't do that, she..."

"You would say that. She's your girlfriend."

"Woah, let's all calm down for a minute," Stephen interrupted.

"Calm down? What the..."

"Yes, calm down. Stop blaming each other for this and think clearly. There were no marks on her body John, correct?"

"Correct. Well I didn't check everywhere, but nothing obvious. No wounds I could see."

"So how is she dead?" Carlo said, shrugging.

"We don't know Carlo, but how could Lucy have done anything that quickly without causing a wound?"

"Somebody did."

"Let's wait and see what the doctor says later before we point fingers. She will examine her properly and see if any wounds are hidden. We still have a problem to deal with, maybe a bigger one than we thought. If this is Ricardo then he's flexing his muscles and showing us he can do something like this without being seen."

"If Lucy couldn't have done it, how could Ricardo have done it?"

"We don't know," said Barker, "but...I don't mean to be blunt but...does it actually matter right now? We have to look out for each other and, more importantly, find Ricardo."

"It matters if we want to prevent it happening again," Lucy joined in. "How can we be sure he won't do the same to us all if we don't know how it was done?"

"You're right Lucy, but if we can get to him before he has the chance, we can stop him. We have to be proactive and not sit and wait for him to come to us."

"What did Maria do that could have caused this? There has to be something" said Carlo, not giving up.

"It could have been a heart attack. It happens."

"That's a long shot," said Stephen, "Although she was drinking something when she was sitting by the pool. Could that have anything to do with it?"

"She had a drink in her hand when she went into the bathroom," Barker said, "I thought it was an unusual thing to do for someone going to use the toilet, but everything we're doing right now is unusual so I let it go."

"She was poisoned?" said Lucy.

"Possibly. We won't know until the autopsy."

"They won't do that here John. They'll take her off the ship in Florida tomorrow and send her to better facilities. So in that sense, you're right, it doesn't matter today or tonight. We have to get this done today before we'll know anything more about how she died."

"So assuming you're right," said Carlo, "We watch what we eat or drink? Eat only what you pick up yourself from the buffet, and don't get served drinks from the bar – ask for bottles and watch them open them, or use the water and juice dispensers."

"And look after Carlo," Lucy added, "You're the only one left who knows what Ricardo actually looks like."

Chapter 35

In a corner of the coffee shop on the lower floor of the Atrium on Deck Five a couple sat drinking cappuccinos by a window looking out over the ocean on the starboard side of the ship, watching the waves gently wash hypnotically against the hull and marvelling at the size of the vessel. They were generally anonymous: early middle age, average build, no real distinguishing features, and dressed in a way that suggested they were trying to be casual but not really succeeding, at least in this particular environment. A couple of fish in not quite the right water. If you were to get up close though you would see more signs. The woman's just-past-the-shoulder pony-tailed hair was expensively cut and coloured, along with immaculately manicured nails and simple clear varnish. Her designer jeans looked ordinary from a distance but were tailored to her curves. The man wore a simple, printed casual shirt that could look normal to a passerby but was also not off-the-peg. His shoes were brown brogues that looked anonymous but were made by an expensive English shoemaker. Unusual cruise wear.

John Barker might have noticed these clues about a couple whose years of good living had made them forget how to look ordinary, but he was otherwise occupied.

"I'm looking forward to getting this done," said the woman,

"Get the fee, deliver the goods, and leave them to it."

"I agree. Where do we meet them?" the man replied.

"Well we know they are one male and one female, crew not passengers, but we don't know where they work or what they look like, so how do we pick a location? We only have a mobile number."

"The boss had the goods dumped in the engineering stores, so my bet is one of them works in engineering."

"We can't go down there though can we?"

"No. So if he's the engineer we'll leave him down below and bring her up here. She shows us the payment and if we're happy we tell him where to find the pallet. When he confirms, she hands over the fee and we put it in the safe and spend our commission."

"Spend it? What straight away? On the ship?"

"Yes, it's the safest way. I have an appointment with our contact in the jewellers this evening. We exchange our two diamonds for cash, then you buy a ring or a necklace, I buy a particular brand of watch. The value is preserved, the shop staff are happy, and once we've handed the payment over in the morning we don't risk losing anything. We just look like we had a good night in the casino."

"You've got it all worked out. So we still haven't decided where."

"Hmmm. She might be in uniform or at least recognisable even if she's off duty, so it's not easy. Maybe we let her choose. It doesn't really matter to us. It'll make her feel safer too."

The woman picked her phone up off the table and began to type out a message to the mobile number. She kept it brief.

Choose the location. In a public area. Female only. 6pm.

Chapter 36

Mary Tkachuk was back in her office when the phone pinged. She shuddered when she saw 'Female only'. Why would they want to do that? And why so early? She'd arranged a disciplinary meeting for 5.45. That wouldn't give her time so she'd have to cancel it. Maybe she could ask Gloria to do it. She'd been working her way up the ladder for a year or so now and it was only a minor thing. She was the person's supervisor anyway, and it could be done in this office for a bit more gravitas. Yes, that would work.

Why would they let me choose the location? She thought. They are obviously from outside, not working already on the ship. So they wouldn't have passes for crew areas. They'd be conspicuous. Not that a little side meeting in a corridor would be too noticeable. It goes on here and there. Also, passengers get lost. God knows how, but they do. It could just look like she was telling them off and how to get back to the main part of the ship.

No, a public place was best for both sides, although she didn't know how many of them there would be. Probably a couple. A single man would be too weird, but a single woman might work. She'd seen a family do it before. That was strange. But kids are easily distracted by phones and don't give a damn about who mum and dad's new friends are. And they provide the perfect cover. Who's going to suspect a family on holiday?

So where could it be? It would have to be somewhere open for safety but with a corner where they could chat without being overheard. She'd have to show them a small bag of diamonds and there are cameras everywhere. *Wait a minute...* she remembered the staff rotas on her wall and looked at the Future Cruises desk. Amanda was due to finish her shift at 6.30. She could go and relieve her early before Inga came on duty. She hated Inga, a textbook Swedish blond, stunning looks, intelligent, and a nice personality to top it off. She was on her way up the ladder too and there wasn't much Mary could do to stop it. But the plan would work. The Future Cruises desk is rarely packed, not at this point on the first or in this case, the only, day of the cruise.

Mary considered ringing Ramirez to discuss it with him but why should she? She was the one taking the risk so she got to decide this time. She texted the words '*Future Cruise desk*' back to the number the message had arrived from. That's all it needed and she didn't expect a reply. These kinds of communications were risky at the best of times. Keep it brief. Facts only. Then she messaged Ramirez to tell him where she was going and to wait for further instructions. He wouldn't be happy about the time being during his shift. He probably had his head in some problem he hoped to solve before then, but he'd have to get used to the idea. The deal needed to be done.

Chapter 37

On the sun deck overlooking the bow Barker, Lucy, Carlo and Stephen were sitting in semi-stunned silence as they each reflected on what had just happened to Maria by the pool. The wind had died down and the sun was providing a last blast of warmth before heading for the horizon in just over an hour's time.

"I just never expected anything to happen to her," Carlo said shaking his head, "She always seemed to find a way out of whatever situation she got into."

"Tell me about it," said Lucy. Carlo gave her a hard stare. "I didn't mean it like that but I do have the wound to prove it. I was just beginning to like her despite our differences." Carlo turned away and said nothing.

"Where do we go from here?" said Stephen.

"I have an idea," said Lucy, "Maria and I discussed it briefly in the lift on the way up to the Lido. We agreed we'd try two things. One was her getting into the pool. We were sure that would work. The other was me singing with the band in the Atrium. They're on in about an hour."

"Are you sure about that?" Stephen sounded concerned, "It didn't work out well for Maria."

"I'm not sure about that either Lucy," added Barker, "Besides, why would Ricardo be lured out to see you?"

"Thanks, John."

"I didn't mean it like that."

"Curiosity killed the cat. And it might just kill Ricardo too. I'll get it added to the schedule online. I'll be surprised if he isn't keeping tabs on that to see what's going on and where. I don't suppose he thinks I'm important but he might not be able to help himself. Besides, he'll know what we're doing and that we're all going to be there. I'm listening if anyone has any other ideas, but this has to be worth a try."

"Talking of killing cats, what are we going to do if we do manage to find him?" said Carlo, "We can't just beat him to death in the middle of the Atrium, although right now I'd really like to. I feel like we're just sitting ducks waiting for him to make a move, and I know that might suit some of you but it isn't good enough for me. I want to find the little shit." Carlo screwed his fists up, his knuckles going white.

"Well on this occasion I'll be singing, so you gentlemen will have to follow him if you see him. Then the easiest thing to do would be to throw him overboard."

"Not good enough. The sneaky bastard would probably survive. I want to see his last breath leave him."

"We'll think of something when we see him," said Stephen, "But I'm not convinced this is a good idea."

"Why not?" said Lucy.

"It just seems hit and miss. There's no guarantee he will come. If he does only Carlo will recognise him. And it's high risk for you, Lucy. Is there no other way?"

"We have to try all ways," said Carlo. "We'll all be there watching. Ricardo isn't going to want to get caught and the whole of the Atrium will be looking at Lucy. She's the safest of all of us. Just don't drink anything."

"That's settled then. I'll go and speak to the band, tell them I'm feeling better, and suggest I do the next set with them. I haven't got long and I need to get changed."

"How are you going to do that?" asked Barker.

"I'll go back to my room and get...ah, no, I see what you mean. Maybe I won't."

"None of us should leave public spaces now unless we're following you-know-who, and we should at least have sight of one other person so we can keep an eye out for each other."

"That doesn't solve my problem."

"No, I know. Can you get someone to go and get your clothes for you?"

"Bit creepy John. No, actually, I can. One of the room stewards can do it for me. They have master keys that will let them in. They can bring something to the disabled toilet near the Atrium and I can get changed in there. First I've got to get hold of the band. Normally I'd go and look in the crew mess just before a set because they'll usually be eating, but this time I'll message them. I think I have Mark's number. He always has his phone with him until he starts playing."

Lucy scrolled through her contacts and wandered around as she typed out a message to Mark. Barker walked closer to Carlo and said, "I want you to go with her to the Atrium and watch out for her when she gets ready."

"OK," said Carlo, "I assumed you'd want to go, but OK."

"I do want to go Carlo, but you can protect her better if he turns up. I like to think I could but...well I'm not built for it like you."

Carlo nodded and explained the plan to Lucy as Barker walked away with Stephen.

Chapter 38

As Mary sat back down at her desk after working out the rota timings her phone pinged again. What was the matter? Were they not happy with the location? But the message was not from the same number. Her phone had two SIM cards, one for work, one for *other* work. The second had no contact names stored in it in case she lost it so it was just a plain number with no identifying information. But she'd seen it before and it made her nervous. It was from the buyer. The person who was organising the handover tomorrow. They were never actually supposed to meet. They would just communicate at each step and confirm they were all happy. Nevertheless, this buyer's reputation preceded him. He did not tolerate failure. Mary was a tough cookie but did not want to upset him.

The message read: *Is it done?*

"No, of course it's not done," Mary said out loud to herself, "We have until tomorrow. What does it matter to you when we do it as long as it's before we dock?" Taking a deep breath in and out she composed herself and messaged back: *Almost.* She banged her phone down on her desk and tried to pick up some of the paperwork she'd been dealing with before the first message came in.

Another message arrived: *Bring it forward*

Mary swore at the phone when she read it. Her instinct was to reply straight back with 'Why?', but knew she had to control her temper. This wasn't a man to mess with and they didn't want to screw up this deal. It was their best chance of an escape from this life and she couldn't be the one to blow it. Clearly, the buyer is getting twitchy about something, but what? What was so important that couldn't wait. How would he even know if she was telling the truth or not if he was sat waiting in Florida for the shipment?

She thought for a minute and then typed *5pm?* into her phone and sent it to the first number, the people collecting the money. This time she put the phone on her desk and sat watching it.

In the coffee shop in the Atrium the couple with the expensive clothes had just ordered more drinks after realising the Future Cruises desk was just across the deck they were already on at the bottom of the Atrium so they had plenty of time before collecting their fee. They were surprised when their mobile bleeped again to indicate a message had arrived. They remembered their training and ignored it for thirty seconds in case the sender was watching and looking for the instant reaction that would identify them. Eventually, they picked the phone up and read it.

"Why would they want to do that? What difference does it make?" said the woman.

The man shrugged, "Does it make any difference to us?"

"Makes me nervous. Aren't we supposed to be in control?"

"They're our buyers. They don't have to go ahead at all if they don't want to."

"But if they pull out we're stuck with a pallet full of product that we have to get off at the other end, and no buyer."

"Well, we could leave it there and find another buyer. They're like buses..."

"And how would you explain that to the supplier?"

"Good point. Let's just get it done when she wants and then we can relax."

The woman confirmed the time with Mary and blew into the froth of her second cappuccino.

Chapter 39

Lucy was a little surprised that Barker had left her alone with Carlo again, but supposed he had something else to do before they all gathered in the Atrium for her show. She realised it was also likely to be due to Carlo's physical attributes and his knowledge of Ricardo's appearance and habits, that Barker thought he was best placed to protect her. There wasn't much conversation as they both walked down the stairs onto the Lido Deck and towards the lifts in the centre of the ship. Carlo just silently scanned the area around them keeping his eyes open for threats. It made Lucy feel strange but safe at the same time.

Lucy stopped before they got to the lifts and motioned for Carlo to step to one side away from the few people passing by.

"Carlo, I didn't harm Maria," said Lucy, "I know you think I did and I don't know how to convince you except to say I didn't hate her enough to kill her. I'm not that kind of person. You come from a different world to me. In your world people settle scores by violence but that's not the case everywhere. Look at me. I'm not built for fighting. I have other talents, but I don't see violence as a solution."

"Except for Ricardo," said Carlo.

Lucy rolled her eyes and said, "Except for Ricardo. But I'm in that with you and the others. If he was just after me I would probably just run and hope for the best."

"And end up dead."

"Maybe, yes."

"So some problems need violent solutions?"

"This one does, yes. But if I can accept that, can you accept that other people don't always do that? That I didn't need to get revenge on Maria for shooting me?"

"I'm here aren't I? Protecting you?"

"Yes. And I'm grateful."

"For my capacity for violence?"

"For your ability to protect me *from* violence. There's a difference. You said so yourself." Lucy gave a wry smile. Carlo nodded blankly, walked over to the lifts and pressed the down arrow.

In the lift, Lucy checked her phone and saw a message from Mark:

Good to hear you're feeling better. Would love to see you for the set at five-thirty.

Meet ten minutes before to go through playlist?

Lucy replied confirming she would see the boys in the Atrium then, after she'd got changed.

The lift continued gliding silently down, dropping below the pool, past some decks made up of just passenger staterooms, and then into the top of the Atrium at Deck Eight, where it stopped to pick a few more people up before going on its way down again.

The Atrium itself was only half full, given the reduced number of passengers and the fact that half of them were on the upper decks in the sun or water, or were feeding themselves in the buffet even at this point in the afternoon. Lucy wondered if this would ever become her normal routine again after today.

Carlo silently glared out through the glass side of the elevator, watching the seating areas on each of the decks as they passed.

On Deck Five the doors opened and the people who had got in with them stepped out again. Lucy and Carlo followed but turned left to the port side of the ship where they would find the disabled toilet in a corner off the main corridor. A few weeks ago Lucy would've taken her time and talked to a few people on her way and been recognised as she went. But this time she was glad these passengers didn't yet know who she was, so she could weave her way through anonymously and stand to one side in the corridor and wait for her clothes to arrive. She hoped it wouldn't be long as, despite their rapprochement, Carlo was a man of few words at the best of times, and she didn't know how much time they could spend looking like a couple who should be enjoying themselves but clearly weren't, before it became uncomfortable. But then, she supposed, they were there to draw attention to themselves. Just maybe not right now.

After about ten minutes of agonisingly stilted conversation and wishing she could make herself temporarily invisible, Lucy noticed a member of the crew walking towards them carrying a long zipped clothes cover on a hanger, weaving his way between passengers looking for somewhere to sit. He smiled when he saw Lucy and gave her an awkward hug as Carlo took the hanger from him.

"Lucy, how are you? I haven't seen you in ages. Are you singing? I asked Angela to help me choose something for you. I hope it's OK? How come you couldn't go to your room?"

"Thanks, Sandro, it's a long story," said Lucy, unzipping the top of the carrier being held uncomfortably by Carlo, "That looks fine. And you even brought shoes. I forgot to ask about them. Thank Angela for me will you?"

Noticing Mark and Philipe walking over to the piano on the opposite side of the Atrium, Lucy saw the opportunity to have a normal conversation and skipped away without a second thought for Carlo, standing near the toilets looking like a bouncer outside an ultra-expensive clothes shop waiting for his employer to relieve his embarrassment.

Carlo instinctively wanted to follow her but Lucy remained in sight all the time, looking animated as she greeted her friends and discussed what they would play for her to sing to. He took the chance to scan around the floor they were on but could only see what was going on down one side of the room due to the people passing and gathering on both sides.

A couple of minutes later Lucy walked confidently back over to Carlo, thanked him for waiting, and took the hanger off him into the large disabled toilet nearby. She was always impressed by the standard of cleanliness on the cruise ships she'd worked on – this one in particular as it was so new. Despite the made-up horror stories online and in the papers, the crew really did try to keep things spotless. It looked cleaner than her own room but at the end of the day it was still a toilet, shared with other people. So Lucy took great care hanging up the garment bag on the only hook on the wall opposite the door. To her left was the actual toilet and sink and associated railings and brackets to help wheelchair users. To her right was a huge mirror the width of the room with a bench below it and a fold-out nappy-changing platform. Not ideal as a dresser but if it was clean it would do.

Angela, one of the cleaning staff who Lucy had met in the crew mess a few months ago had done a good job of picking Lucy an outfit and even remembered her make-up bag. It only had the basics in, as the rest of it was sprawled across the tiny table in front of the mirror in her room, but this would do the job for today. Lucy unzipped the garment bag and picked out the shoes and make-up bag and put them in front of the mirror. She felt weird not having a shower before getting changed for a show, but that was out of the question today, so she undressed and rolled up her jeans and jumper and dropped them into the bottom of the garment bag before slipping the inky blue dress off the hanger and putting it on, followed by matching shoes. It was a subtle choice for an afternoon performance rather than a livelier evening show that would justify something a bit more extravagant. Lucy applied just enough make-up, put everything back in the bag and zipped it up.

Chapter 40

Amanda Ryan from Freemantle in Australia was having a quiet day working on the Future Cruises desk. Day one of a cruise was often quiet and this was no exception, so she was looking forward to the end of this particular shift and a busier day tomorrow when the ship filled up for a fortnight's trip to the Caribbean. While she was filling in some enquiry forms from passengers, she heard a familiar voice coming from someone walking into the open-plan office in a corner just off the Atrium on the opposite side to the coffee shop.

"Hi Amanda, how's it been today?" said Mary Tkachuk in a brighter-than-usual tone.

"Oh, Hi Mary! Er, good thanks. Some good enquiries, just not particularly busy as you'd expect with the lower numbers and the good weather," Amanda smiled back at Mary.

"I thought I'd come over and let you get off. I've got some reports to run from your PC so you might as well have an early finish as I've got to be here anyway. No need for both of us to be hanging around."

"Oh, OK..." said Amanda, surprised at the generous offer. She'd worked well for Mary up until now but had heard she could be strict and ruthless if necessary, and she wasn't normally the chatty type. But an extra hour or so off was a bonus she wasn't going to turn down so she started tidying her desk before thanking Mary again and walking away from the Atrium towards the nearest lift.

Mary watched Amanda walk away as she sat down at the PC and tried her best to look like she was doing some real work, but actually just opened and closed a few windows and printed off a random page of figures that meant nothing in particular but helped with the illusion if anyone was watching. She was also nervous, which was not a familiar feeling for her. She had worked hard and become confident in her abilities, and she knew her job inside out. But since she had teamed up with Ramirez and started doing these deals, at first for others but now for themselves, she felt a little less in control.

It didn't help that in her trouser pocket she had a black velvet bag about the size of a folded handkerchief that contained just under or just over two million US dollars worth of diamonds, depending on which jeweller you asked and in which port. That fact alone made her feel extremely vulnerable, although she and Ramirez had been very careful to keep quiet about what they were doing and where they went when they were off the ship. Neither of them was the talkative type, which might've meant them slipping up and revealing details of their plan. They were the ideal couple for keeping secrets. Few people would pry into their private lives. There should be no reason for anything to go wrong.

A woman wandered over into the area in front of the desk and browsed a few of the leaflets on display regarding other ships and asked Mary a couple of questions about the itinerary of a particular cruise on Starlight's sister ship Twilight next July in the Mediterranean. Mary was easily capable of doing most of these types of jobs around the ship, so was able to notice out of the corner of her eye a couple walking into the area behind the first woman who was now asking about discounts. Mary looked at the clock on the wall. It was dead on 5pm. That couldn't be coincidence could it? She answered the woman as politely but briefly as she could and said, "I'll be with you in a moment," to the couple that had just arrived.

Happy with her discount the woman walked away almost convinced to book, but said she would speak to her husband and come back later. Mary's heart beat faster and jumped a bit when she realised she'd not thought of how to identify whoever she was handing over the payment to. That was a bit of an oversight, she thought, but then they hadn't confirmed how that should happen either, so she had to think on her feet. She wandered over to the couple who had sat themselves down at one of the two tables along the wall of windows overlooking the sea and were watching the sun finally setting. That in itself was unusual. Normally those tables were where they would take someone who had made a serious enquiry and sounded like they were ready to book something if they could just dot the i's and cross the t's. This couple may well have come in to discuss something other than a cruise.

As she approached the middle-aged couple Mary noticed the quality of their clothes and the woman's haircut. Not too unusual: you get people from all sorts of backgrounds on cruise ships, but these two were no strangers to money. This made her squirm a little at the thought of handing over a fortune to them, although she knew they would only be getting a tiny cut from the supplier.

"Good evening," said Mary, in her best professional voice, "Have you come to make a payment?" It was as close a question as she could think of to ask without being weird if it turned out these were not the people she was waiting for.

The couple looked at each other before the man said, "No. But we are here to receive a payment." Both of them looked directly into Mary's eyes for signs of recognition. They clearly weren't as careful as she was about saying something that could be confusing if Mary hadn't turned out to be the one with the diamonds.

"I understand," said Mary, taking a seat at the low coffee table opposite them. The couple had decided to sit as far into the office as they could with their backs facing the corner, so they could see out into the Atrium where the band were assembling to give one of their performances. Mary sat opposite, side-on to the Atrium, so couldn't see as easily what was happening. "You're expecting a payment from me?"

"Mmhmm," said the man and woman at the same time, nodding at her.

"Can I get you a coffee?" said Mary suddenly standing up and walking back around the desk to mess with the small drinks machine.

"No thanks, we've had plenty," said the man, looking a little confused.

Mary returned with what might have been a freshly poured coffee for herself, but was in fact an empty cup which she put down on the table in front of her, further confusing the couple. She then slid an acrylic leaflet holder to the right-hand end of the table so that it would hide what she was about to show them. Reaching into her pocket she removed the fabric bag. Glancing quickly to her right to make sure there was nobody else nearby she tipped it up and let the contents drop out onto a notepad in front of her. The couple's eyes focussed intently on the diamonds but they were otherwise unmoved. It was clear they'd done this before and were used to concealing their emotions.

Almost immediately Mary pushed one small diamond forward towards the man, cupped her hand around the remainder and slid them back across the notepad into the empty cup she was holding below the table's edge, making a momentary tinkling sound. She was pleased with her quick thinking in finding a way to have the diamonds on the table but not so obvious if someone approached. She'd assumed the man would check the sample she left on the table but in the blink of an eye, the woman picked it up and glanced around before lifting it closer. Of course: a woman who knows her diamonds.

Chapter 41

Lucy walked around the back of the glass elevators to get to the other side of the Atrium where the boys were just about ready to go and looked like they were relieved to see her. She was a couple of minutes behind schedule.

"Must admit I was getting nervous. How're you feeling?" said Sam, one of the guitarists.

"Really good thanks," Lucy lied, worried about her nerves showing, "What have you got for me?"

The musicians gathered round and showed Lucy a short set list they'd prepared for her. They'd kept it simple, using songs they'd played many times before that they knew she would have no trouble with if she was still feeling a bit rough.

"Try to give us a bit of notice if you've got to run to the loo," Mark said with a grin.

Lucy laughed back at him, "You think you're funny?"

The band began with a number that had a decently long intro so that the audience would have a few seconds to realise they'd started, settle into their seats and quieten down a little. There was a decent number of them, thought Lucy, considering the warm afternoon, but it had just started to go dark outside so it seemed like they'd all headed in here. It was her job to keep them entertained.

Lucy was able to look around as she sang, seemingly moving to the rhythm and emotion of the music, but at the same time she was trying to spot her guardians: Barker, Carlo and Stephen. She had no idea where they would be standing or even whether she would be able to spot them at all. They might hide in the background so that Ricardo would have no distractions if he showed up. She thought she should feel more nervous than she did about being the bait, but had no choice but to get on with the job and let the others worry about that. She owed it to Maria to do whatever she could to catch him.

One deck above, Barker watched Lucy take the stage, moved backward away from the railings, and walked through a bar that partly encircled this half of the Atrium on Deck Six. He remembered something his brother, a wedding photographer, had said to him about photographing wedding speeches: take a few photos of those speaking, then turn the other way and watch the audience for their reactions. Ricardo's reaction was likely to be different. All he had to do was spot it.

Barker could see Stephen on Deck Seven above and on the other side of the Atrium, keeping each other in sight at all times like they'd planned. But he worried that he couldn't see Carlo on Deck Five below. He was supposed to be closest to Lucy in case of danger and it made him nervous, but he couldn't change the plan now without knowing why Carlo had deviated from it. Maybe he was just out of sight under the overhanging floor. Maybe Carlo could see Stephen but not Barker and everything was OK. He wished they all had those invisible earplugs and microphones they all used in spy films so they could all keep in touch, but remembered thinking how ridiculous they'd all sound talking to themselves in the crowd.

Chapter 42

In the corner of the Future Cruises area, the woman had examined the diamond Mary had given her and dropped it into the cup on the table with the others.

"That's my end of the deal. Now we need to see the goods," said Mary seriously.

The couple looked at each other and gave a confirmatory nod before turning back to Mary.

"Tell your friend to go to the engineering stores," said the man, maintaining eye contact with Mary. He had done this several times before but this was his least favourite part of the deal because, having not loaded the goods themselves, it relied on him having been given accurate information as to their whereabouts. If anything was wrong with the details it could spook the buyer and the deal could be off with the goods left stranded on the ship and the chances of retrieving them very slim. That would not please their supplier. At the very least they would not be asked to work for him again. But if they lost a shipment and had nothing to show for it...well they might as well jump overboard instead of docking in the morning. He consoled himself with the thought that all parties involved wanted this to go smoothly so would do their utmost to make it happen.

Mary waited for a reply to arrive from Ramirez about the information she'd just sent him. He quickly sent the words: *On my way.* Then a couple of minutes later, *What now?*

"He's there," said Mary, trying to use phrases that wouldn't sound odd to passers-by, "What next?"

Chapter 43

In the stores, Ramirez wandered awkwardly round the room scanning for likely containers or crates and waiting for more instructions from the suppliers. What was keeping them? He had no idea what form this shipment would take, as it always varied to keep the authorities guessing. He had the power to look wherever he wanted but was aware it would seem strange to anyone else if they saw him opening random pallets, particularly if someone walked in to see him open a crate full of suspicious packets of powder. Right on cue, a junior engineer walked in and, seeing Ramirez, mumbled something about a faulty electrical cabinet in the laundry and asked if he knew where he could find spare circuit breakers. Ramirez climbed out from behind a crate and showed the man the cupboard full of electrical parts. The man looked like he wanted to ask more questions but suddenly seemed to remember that Ramirez wasn't one for small talk. Satisfied, he took the breaker from Ramirez and left.

Mary breathed in and out steadily as she sat staring at the man and woman, waiting for more instructions, but none came.

"What the hell is *he* doing here?!" the man growled suddenly but quietly, looking out at the people watching Lucy and her band, "Are you working for him?"

"What? Who...?" said Mary turning to try to see who they were looking at.

"Him!" said the man, pointing at the crowd.

Mary looked out along the row of people standing watching the band. All were facing away from her but only one was moving. A short, dark-haired, young male was walking away from her, keeping one eye on the performance as he left the room. Mary felt sick as she realised who it was. Ricardo Gutierrez was on board Starlight. Her face flushed and the hairs on the back of her neck stood up. She decided she would play it cool and pretend not to know who they were referring to. How did they know who Ricardo was? Because they were in the same line of business of course. These are the risks when you try to trade with a rival cartel. As she turned back she saw the couple were standing up looking like they were getting ready to leave.

"But...What..?" she said as the couple started to move out from behind the table, "Where are you going?"

"Deal's off," the woman said, "You've set us up."

"Set you up? I..." Mary began before watching the woman lunge towards the coffee table and try to grab the cup containing the diamonds. Being smaller and quicker, Mary reacted faster and reached the cup at the same time, but the struggle only succeeded in spilling the diamonds all over the floor

Mary's phone pinged with the message: *Where is it?* but she wasn't in a position to answer. The diamonds were on the carpet and the man and woman opposite leapt around the coffee table down onto the floor to grab what they could. Mary pocketed a small handful before the man grabbed her and pulled her away while the woman helped herself to the rest. Mary had to fight the instinct to shout out for the help that she would normally expect to come if she was being attacked, but this was a fight she couldn't draw any attention to for obvious reasons. The crowd was facing the other way watching Lucy and her band, so nobody saw a thing.

"Where is it?" Mary said angrily, "The shipment, where is it?"

The woman stood up again and walked away, ignoring the question, while the man stood in front of Mary until his partner had disappeared through the crowd.

"Don't follow us. Don't speak to us. If either of us sees you again we'll make sure security finds it before you do."

Chapter 44

As Lucy finished one song and began another she was aware of a disturbance on the edge of the crowd but nothing that worried her enough to break stride. It was probably just someone arguing over a chair or complaining to the staff about something. Nobody in the watching audience seemed that bothered about it either so she ignored it and carried on.

Barker watched from the deck above. He could see over the crowd and noticed the fuss coming from the Future Cruises area. One man walked past it, three people ran out of it, voices were raised. It piqued his suspicion enough to decide to go down and take a look. Carlo should be on the spot but he still couldn't be seen. Two people pushed through the audience and crossed the dance floor in front of Lucy, failing to keep a low profile. A woman in a crew uniform went left out of the Atrium and a dark-haired man went to the right. The only one of those that should really cause concern right now was the latter, so Barker indicated to Stephen on the deck above to take his place and keep Lucy in sight as he walked down the nearest staircase on the port side of the Atrium.

As Barker walked round the back of the glass elevators behind the stage where Lucy was performing he saw the feet of a man entering one of the two lifts, and the doors closing behind him.

He pressed the nearest call button to see if it would open the doors again, with no luck. He ran around the back of the crowd past the Future Cruises desk so he could watch the glass elevator go up. Only one person was in it, a slim, dark-haired man aged about thirty, with a self-satisfied expression, looking out over the Atrium as he ascended to Deck Eight where the lift stopped and he turned round and stepped out. Barker couldn't be sure it was Ricardo but it was the closest likeness he'd seen all day so had to be worth following. He ran back around and into an empty lift near the one he'd seen Ricardo in, whose doors had just begun to close after a family had walked out of it. He stuck his hand between the doors and the sensor opened them again. This lift wasn't glass, so he couldn't see anything as he went up. He pressed the button for Deck Eight and the button to close the doors and waited for it to move. Less than ten seconds later the doors opened on Deck Eight and Barker jumped out, half-expecting to see Ricardo waiting for him, but of course he was gone. There was no sign of him down the corridor to the staterooms so Barker walked purposefully around the piano bar on the starboard side of the Atrium. It was busy with drinkers soaking up the atmosphere of the performance of the band three decks below, but the majority were couples and families so he could see clearly that Ricardo wasn't here and continued round to the photo gallery on the other side of the ship.

Barker sighed as he completed the full circle of the top deck of the Atrium, reaching the glass elevators again where he'd started. He debated whether to run down one of the stateroom corridors to see if he could catch Ricardo unawares, but realised that could be what Ricardo expected him to do. He could be waiting at any of the door alcoves Barker would have to run past. He'd be a fool to do that without backup and he couldn't signal Stephen for help as that would leave Lucy vulnerable, so he got into the elevator that he'd seen Ricardo use and went back down to Deck Five.

Lucy was halfway through her set so Barker quietly turned right out of the elevator and circled the Atrium clockwise through the coffee shop, conscious that he looked like the policeman he'd trained to be, always looking for suspects. As he approached the corner before the Future Cruises desk he noticed Mary Tkachuk rushing in the other direction, almost breaking into a run. Given that the last time he'd seen her she'd been running away from the scene of Ernesto's demise, he wondered whether she'd seen the same thing he had.

Chapter 45

In the relatively empty Explorers Lounge on Deck Seven, away from the noise of the Atrium, the well-dressed, drug-dealing couple sat down on a sofa facing an empty stage where a couple of technicians were setting up microphones and moving a piano ready for a performance later in the evening. A female bartender came over to ask if they wanted to order any drinks. They both sat in silence for five minutes until she came back with a gin and tonic and a large whiskey with ice. The man was still shaking, out of anger rather than fear.

"I told you we shouldn't have got involved in this run. We've been busted piling in on another gang's territory. And by that little sneak too."

"We don't know that. It could've been a coincidence. Don't you think he'd have done something if he'd seen us? We got most of the payment, enough to pay the supplier. She has a problem on her hands now, ours are clean. She's going to be frantically searching that store room all night trying to find the product. It'll take them hours and they have to get it off the ship in the morning or their buyer will be very unhappy. Besides, remember what I heard this morning?"

"About Ernesto?"

"Yes."

"We don't know if that's true. What would his son be doing here tonight if that had happened?"

"I don't know. I don't really care. What matters is he's here and he's trapped."

"Trapped?"

"Yes, trapped."

"I'm not following."

"He can't go anywhere until tomorrow morning. If Ernesto is dead Ricardo is his successor...alone, without his entourage."

"Surely he wouldn't be on here without help?"

"You'd think not but he wasn't being followed through the Atrium by half a dozen armed guards like he usually would be was he? He's as vulnerable this evening as he's ever likely to be. This is an opportunity we might never get again."

"You mean...?"

"Why not?"

"How do we find him?"

"Maybe we make him find us."

Chapter 46

As Lucy finished the last song she thanked the audience for their generous applause and felt relieved she'd got through it and nothing bad seemed to have happened while she was working. Although maybe that meant their plan hadn't worked. She scanned the floors above for any signs of Barker or Stephen and looked around on Deck Five, but didn't notice either of them. Was that good or bad? The whole idea of her appearance had been to provoke some kind of reaction. On the one hand, she was glad she was still in one piece, but on the other frustrated that they were no further on in ending this hopeless situation.

She thanked Mark, Philipe and Sam for a great performance and chatted animatedly about what they thought had gone well and what they might do in tomorrow's schedule. She desperately wanted to share her secret with them, even to tell the whole ship what was going on so they could all look out for this man. As she put the microphone back on its stand she realised she had the power to do that. Surely that would be the fastest way to find him if everyone knew? But then he'd hide in the crew areas, or he would have help on board who would warn him or do his dirty work for him and they'd actually be no better off.

As the boys tidied the stage and packed away their instruments Lucy noticed Stephen walking across the dance floor weaving between the people who had got up and were about to go and find a drink or something to eat. She felt awkward when she instinctively smiled at him but toned it down with a simple question: "Anything?"

Stephen shook his head, "No, nothing. But John asked me to swap places with him so he could go and look at something, so I don't know what was going on. I heard a bit of noise down here but couldn't see anything from where I was.

"I heard that too," said Lucy, "Didn't seem to amount to much but you never know."

Barker appeared around the side of the stage but Lucy didn't smile this time because she could tell by his expression he had something to say, "What happened?"

"Let's sit down in the coffee shop for a minute so I can tell you."

"Wait, where's Carlo?"

"I thought he was with you."

"He was with me when I got changed over there," Lucy pointed toward the corner of the Atrium where she'd changed in the disabled toilet, "I need to go and see if he's still there."

"We'll come with you. Until we know where he is we need to stick together."

All three walked around the back of the Atrium past the glass elevators. No sign of Carlo. The toilet was engaged for a minute or so until an elderly woman opened the door and walked out, startled to find Stephen, Barker and Lucy looking at her.

"Sorry! Desperate!" said Lucy and shuffled past into the toilet, leaving Barker and Stephen looking like they were in the queue.

Three or four minutes later Lucy emerged having changed

back into her jeans and T-shirt and hung up her dress back in the garment bag on the hanger and left it inside, "Normally I'd want this put back in my room straight away, but tonight I think I'll pass. Have you seen him?"

"No," said Barker, "He might have gone walkabout looking for you know who, thinking you were safe with us keeping an eye out for you." Barker put his arm round Lucy's back and ushered her over towards the coffee shop where they could sit down and take stock. Stephen went to the counter and ordered some drinks.

"I think I saw Ricardo," said Barker when the three of them found a table in the far corner and sat down.

"What?" Lucy replied, "When?"

"Just now, about ten minutes ago."

"Where was he?" asked Stephen.

"In one of the lifts going up to Deck Eight. I followed him but I was too late to see where he went."

"Why didn't you tell me?"

"I thought about it but that would have taken even longer and Lucy would have had no cover. It could've been an attempt to get us away from her, or to trick me into following."

"It might have been a diversion to get Carlo," said Lucy, gazing into space in front of her, "I don't get how that could happen."

"How do you mean?"

"Well how can a scrawny little git like Ricardo physically deal with Carlo? He must've had help."

"This isn't working. We need to stay together from now on. He's picking us off one by one."

"And he's started with the big ones, the ones that know him, and know how he works. He's not as useless as we'd hoped."

133

Chapter 47

Mary stormed into her office, slammed the door behind her, and threw herself down into the chair behind her desk, head spinning at what had just happened. She knew she shouldn't have met them on her own. She'd put herself at a disadvantage and paid the price, literally. They'd made off with three-quarters of the diamonds and she didn't know where the product was, except that it was in the engineering stores somewhere. Or was it? They could easily have been lying, testing her and Ramirez out. Maybe they were going to send him somewhere else afterwards where the product really was. She began to panic inside. The buyer was expecting the goods tomorrow. They had barely twelve hours to find it and it could be anywhere, if it was here at all.

A knock at the door focussed her mind. She was about to say, "I'm busy," when the door opened anyway and Carlo stepped through into the room.

"What was all that about?" he said.

Mary was almost lost for words, "What do you mean?"

"Don't mess with me, Mary. I saw you on the floor of the Future Cruises office being pushed around by a middle-aged couple, fighting over something. Luckily for you, I don't think many other people noticed."

"I've no idea what you're talking about."

"You were dealing, weren't you? Something went wrong."

"I told you, it's nothing to do with you."

"You forget Mary. I know you two. You're a couple of chancers who'll work for anybody. No loyalty. Besides, Ernesto told me you were up to something. He would've been here to see it himself if..." Carlo trailed off.

At that moment Ramirez walked through the door having not heard from Mary since the message telling him to go to the stores, "What happ... what's he doing here?" Ramirez stopped and stared at Carlo.

"He just appeared. He's not the problem."

"He's *a* problem," said Ramirez, turning square on to Carlo as if he might stand a chance of forcing him out of the room if he felt the need to.

"The problem is Ricardo's here," interrupted Mary. Both men turned to look at her.

"Here? On the ship?" said Ramirez.

"You saw him? Where?" added Carlo.

Mary put her hand up to prevent them from peppering her with more questions, "In the Atrium, just before that scuffle you saw." Mary looked at Carlo. Carlo raised his eyebrows.

"That's why you didn't get back to me to tell me where the prod..." Ramirez stopped himself from finishing the sentence in front of Carlo, "Where it was."

"Yes," said Mary, cautiously looking between Ramirez and Carlo trying to decide how much to say.

"Ernesto's dead," said Carlo, thinking they possibly didn't know for sure, but probably should, and that it might make them relax a little and trust him. Mary and Ramirez looked at each other, taking in the new information to decide if it made any difference, and whether to continue the conversation in front of Carlo or to clam up and say nothing more, "But I'm sure you guessed that. You were in the car with us."

"We didn't know for sure," said Ramirez, "We left quickly."

"I noticed. So you don't need to worry about him finding out you're dealing with someone else." There was a pause while Mary and Ramirez looked at each other like guilty children, "That's what's going on here isn't it?"

Mary and Ramirez ignored the question. "So what are *you* doing here?" Mary asked Carlo.

"Avoiding Ricardo but *looking* for Ricardo. He followed us because we killed his father..."

"Who's 'we'?" said Mary, "You didn't kill him. You were standing on the other side of the car. You drove him there. You mean the girl and the cop, and the other guy?"

"And Maria..." Carlo chose not to tell them what had happened to her, at least not yet. Not until he'd got more information out of them.

"I'm not surprised he's followed you if she's here," said Ramirez, "She drove the car into Ernesto. Why didn't you just walk away?"

Carlo briefly explained to them the logic of how Ricardo now wanted to kill all of them because they'd either killed his father, allowed it to happen, or stolen his money, and that the only option was to get rid of him. "And if I were you two I wouldn't assume you are off the hook yet. Especially not after what I've seen tonight."

"You've seen nothing. Nothing but an argument."

"An expensive argument I'm guessing."

Mary and Ramirez looked at each other but said nothing.

"Look I don't give a damn who you're buying stuff from or

selling to. I don't work for Ernesto any more and I'll never work for Ricardo, will I? I'm a free agent. But maybe we can help each other?"

"How'd you figure that out?"

"Well, I'll help you sort your deal out, and you help me...us... sort Ricardo out."

"It would help us find it faster," Mary said to Ramirez.

Ramirez considered the idea for a moment, "I suppose you'll want a cut? You're not having a third. You only just got here."

"I don't want anything. I just want Ricardo."

Ramirez scowled disbelievingly at Carlo, then looked at Mary, "Do you believe that?"

"I want out Ramirez. And to do that I need Ricardo out of the way. Once that's done the shit will hit the fan and you two had better decide quickly who you're working for because if you get in the way of the fight you won't last five minutes."

"We only need to last until tomorrow," said Mary, taking the initiative from Ramirez. "We have a shipment on board we bought from the competition – you know who they are. It was loaded today and we're selling it tomorrow as soon as we dock. I was paying the supplier's brokers when Ricardo walked past and they freaked because they thought they'd walked into a trap. They think Ernesto or Ricardo sent us in deliberately to bring them out of the woodwork to see who he was competing against. Of course, we all know who's who around here, but Ernesto might have wanted to see who was brazen or stupid enough to challenge his authority, and stray onto his patch."

Ramirez took over while Carlo took it all in, "We think it's in the engineering stores. If they were telling the truth up to that point. But that's apparently when Ricardo walked past." He looked at Mary who nodded in confirmation.

"They started to walk away and then maybe they remembered they'd given us an idea of where the stuff was, so made a grab for the diamonds. I panicked and tried to retrieve them because I didn't know if we'd find the shipment. Still don't. If we don't find it by morning we're in big trouble."

"Maybe the fact they made a grab for the diamonds is a good thing," said Ramirez. "Maybe it means the stuff really is in the stores?"

"Or maybe it was just because they saw a woman on her own against the two of them and they tried their luck?" added Carlo.

Ramirez just scowled, "Will you help or won't you?"

Carlo knew his priority should be to help the others, but he'd never trusted Mary and Ramirez. He knew that if they found Ricardo first, they might be persuaded to help him instead. They would work for the highest bidder. So the best thing to do was to keep them onside by helping them find that shipment. The shipment that Ernesto had told him was being loaded this morning in the car before they had picked Mary and Ramirez up. The intention had been to collect the money from Barker, and then interrogate them about who they were dealing with, or to follow them through it and find out that way. When the accident happened Carlo forgot all about it but now had a chance to pick up the search again. They had succeeded this far so they must have friends on board who could keep their eyes and ears open for information.

Chapter 48

Carlo had never been in the crew-only areas of a cruise ship before, or any ship at all for that matter. He'd enjoyed the past couple of days he'd spent with his girlfriend on the short trip to Bimini and back. It had felt like a holiday even though Ernesto had sent him to keep an eye on Barker. That was the good thing about working for Ernesto, if you worked hard and did what he expected he would treat you well. Carlo had thought he might go a long way working for him, but he had seen enough to realise the risk wasn't worth it. He had been paid well and had put aside some money for the future, but soon he would have to make a decision about what to do next. It was tempting to demand a share of whatever Ramirez might get for the shipment they were looking for, but he didn't want to get his hands dirty again. Right now he could walk away clean if he didn't get involved. Opportunities to do that rarely came along in this line of work.

The corridors were busier than he'd expected with different crew members walking purposefully back and forth in different uniforms. Ramirez had found him a boiler suit to wear over his clothes so that he would go unnoticed as they walked down to the engineering stores. It was dirty, old, and too tight, probably one of his own unwashed ones. 'It will look more realistic', Ramirez had told Carlo. Carlo could just smell stale sweat.

Mary stayed in her office for now as she was well known all around the ship for handling the contracts of most of the workers. Almost all of them knew who she was and would wonder what she was doing searching a store room, even though they suspected about her relationship with Ramirez. They wouldn't say anything to either of them but if questioned at a later date by someone wanting to know too much, they might say something incriminating and Ramirez thought it better that he and Carlo handled it for now.

"If anyone asks, you are new to the ship and joined today in Nassau," said Ramirez to Carlo. "No one will question it."

Carlo nodded, not entirely happy to be taking instructions from someone like Ramirez, but choosing to go along with him for now. This was Ramirez's domain and Carlo needed to be invisible, "Yes boss." Ramirez gave him a sideways look but said nothing more.

The store room was bigger and warmer than Carlo expected. On land, this might be a dirty, damp shed tacked on the end of a factory, but here on a ship, it was a metal-walled room not too far from the engine room and with pipes running in all directions across the ceiling. There were cabinets full of tools and manuals, electrical panels on the walls that meant nothing to him, and dozens of pallets, crates, boxes and drums full of spare parts and materials and things going for repair. He didn't know where to start.

"The problem we have," Ramirez said, "Is that this room is open to anyone in the department. They are free to come in and out to look for things they need to do their jobs, so we cannot lock ourselves in. And that's twenty-four-seven. There has just been a shift-change and I've given my teams tasks to do so they should all be busy, but things change so be aware of that."

"Can you tell me where to start looking? Maybe rule out some of this stuff so I don't waste time?"

"Yes. The one we are looking for will have been loaded today..." The door opened and a young technician walked in, acknowledging his boss with a nod, but Ramirez ignored him, picked up a clipboard, and handed it to Carlo, "...So you can check the contents against what we ordered." The technician found what he came for and left again quickly. "Keep that with you. It makes you look like you're doing something official for me rather than poking around on your own."

"You'll be here as well though too?"

"Yes, but I might have to talk to someone if they need help. My office is just next door. I was saying that the containers loaded today are all along that wall," Ramirez pointed to one side of the room, "You can ignore anything over there. At least I think so. I will check myself just to be sure. I take it you know what you're looking for?" Carlo looked at Ramirez with raised eyebrows.

Both men set about examining the fresh boxes and shrink-wrapped pallets, carefully cutting open the packaging and nosying inside. Sometimes they would have to open things right up to get at anything to see what it was, other times the parts were obvious, but Carlo wondered how well things might be hidden. Nothing could be too obvious after all, otherwise it would be easily noticed. And he wasn't familiar with how this supplier worked. They all had different methods. Had it been one of Ernesto's he felt he would have understood where to start. And it wasn't like he could stop and ask Ramirez too many questions in case they were interrupted. They just had to get on with it until they found something.

Chapter 49

Upstairs, Mary Tkachuk couldn't keep still. She was officially off duty although she hardly ever took breaks except for sleep, preferring to keep her finger on the pulse by prowling around the ship, sometimes out of uniform to avoid being too obvious or being stopped and questioned by an employee with a grievance or payment dispute. Knowing what was going on below was preoccupying her but she understood why she couldn't get involved just yet. So she decided to look for Ricardo. It sounded so simple but she of all people was well aware of how big this place was. Needle-in-a-haystack wasn't even close. But she'd seen him walk out of the Atrium in a certain direction and decided to go back and start there. Maybe she would get some inspiration or logic as to where he may have gone.

As she walked she couldn't help but imagine the dreams that would come true if they pulled this off, if they found the shipment and sold it tomorrow and disappeared into America. They had temporary visas that would allow them to pretend to be tourists for a while, long enough to vanish, change their identities, and start new lives. The money would help with that. But she shuddered when she thought about what would happen if they didn't find anything. No new lives in the land of the free. They had gone to so much trouble risking stealing those diamonds from Ricardo's chandelier so they could pay for this job. The thought that it might all collapse at the final step was too much. And all because you-know-who just happened to turn up at the wrong time in the wrong place.

As she walked past the coffee shop lost in her thoughts she almost bumped into some people who were just leaving and stepped back to let them pass. They didn't move straight away so she looked up and made eye contact.

"Mary?" said Barker, not sure what else to add, not knowing what she knew and didn't know about what had happened since he last saw her running away from Ernesto's smashed-up Jaguar.

"Mr Barker," said Mary after a sharp intake of breath she just about managed to disguise, "Good evening." Mary nodded first at Lucy and then Stephen, the man she knew little about but who seemed to be everywhere.

There was a pregnant pause where Barker and Mary looked at each other with the same questions floating around in their heads, wondering whether to say anything or acknowledge anything more than each other's presence. Mary was being even less forthcoming than usual. Barker wondered where she and Ramirez had gone that morning after the crash and what they had learned since. Mary thought she perhaps knew more than he expected but didn't know whether to acknowledge the fact.

Eventually, the deadlock broke when an expressionless Lucy stepped across Mary as if to head away from her, expecting Barker and Stephen to follow. As they did so Mary took a gamble and said, "Did you see him?" She felt better for getting it off her chest but was nervous about how they would react.

Assuming she could only mean one person, they all looked at

her in surprise for a few seconds before Barker asked, "Ricardo? Yes, I did."

"Where?"

"Deck Eight. He went up in the lift from the Atrium but by the time I got there he'd disappeared."

"You brought him here," Mary stated. Barker couldn't deny it so there was a long pause as they just looked at each other.

"After what happened this morning, wherever we go, he's bound to follow."

"But why here?"

"Because the island is his domain. This is ours. He has limited help here. On the island, he could buy anybody."

"That only gives you until morning."

"Unless we find him first. You could help us."

Mary mulled over in her head how much to share with them about what had happened on her side of the story so far. She certainly wasn't going to mention the drug shipment or the bungled payment, as it didn't seem like Barker had seen any of what went on. She also didn't want to mention Carlo yet even though she knew he had boarded the ship with them and they may be wondering where he was. She should only volunteer the minimum amount of detail about anything so she settled for, "I have no loyalty to Ricardo."

Barker thought, *I doubt you have any loyalty to anyone other than yourself*, but stopped himself from saying it out loud. She could've said a flat 'No' but she hadn't. He got the impression she'd be happy to see the back of Ricardo as well for her own reasons. Maybe she'd crossed him in the past, maybe she was hoping to step into the vacuum if he disappeared, but for now it didn't matter why. The only thing that mattered was finding him.

Chapter 50

"You have no description at all?" said Carlo to Ramirez, starting to open the third new shipment in the store room. The first he'd opened was a crate full of boxes of electrical parts, each of which had to be opened individually and took around an hour to examine. The second was a box of drums containing liquids that had to be opened and checked for secret compartments. Carlo didn't usually get too involved in this side of the business but knew that things could be hidden in the most ingenious and tiniest of places to help evade the border police, so everything needed to be checked if they didn't know where to look.

"Nothing," said Ricardo, "Mary was in the middle of the transaction when he appeared and they got spooked. We don't even know for sure that it's here. They could've been testing us, to see if we'd obey instructions properly before they gave us the full details. It wouldn't be the first time a seller has done that."

"Do you know where they are?"

"Who?"

"The seller's brokers. The couple who took the diamonds."

"They disappeared."

"Maybe we should look for them. Try to get some information out of them."

"I think it's easier to look in here for the product. There is a chance they were telling the truth, but we don't know where they've gone on the ship. If I were them I'd be hiding in a cabin until tomorrow morning. We don't know their names so we can't look them up. If they stay hidden we've got no chance."

"A bit like Ricardo."

"No, he has to make an appearance at some time. His work isn't finished."

"You don't think he'd send someone to do his dirty work?"

"Why get on the ship at all? It's not worth the risk unless he's come to do the job himself."

"Anything over there?" Carlo nodded in the direction of the crates and pallets Ramirez was checking through.

"Nothing. We could be here for a couple more hours at least."

Carlo sighed and returned to his task. The next shipment was a pallet with products shrink-wrapped onto it with banding tying them down. He cut that off with a knife and started peeling back the shrink-wrap from one corner, making sure nothing rolled or dropped off the pallet as he went. There were small and medium-sized boxes of plumbing spares, along with small stacks of pipes of several different diameters, some for supplying water, some for drainage. He rummaged through the boxes of pipe joints, elbows, end-caps and washers, quickly assessing that there was nothing hidden amongst them. The drainage pipes made a hollow plastic sound as he tapped them, indicating they had nothing inside. To be absolutely sure he picked them up and had a quick look through each one to check for light shining through.

When he came to the narrow copper pipes he had to cut away more shrink-wrap wound around bunches of about a dozen lengths held together with tape. *Hmmm, almost as if they don't want you to get at them*, he thought, immediately realising maybe that was deliberate. He slid a handful of pipes out of what was left of the wrapping and looked into one end. Nothing. No light came through. That was a tell-tale sign.

Carlo took a quick glance over at Ramirez who was leaning into a deep crate fishing for whatever was at the bottom. He picked up a screwdriver Ramirez had given him to prize things open and poked it into the end of one of the pipes. There was a soft, plasticky resistance an inch or so inside. He poked again only with more force, this time feeling the resistance pop slightly before letting the screwdriver push further. He checked Ramirez again – he was still occupied. Carlo slid the screwdriver out slowly and looked at it carefully as he put it and the pipes back down on the pallet so Ramirez wouldn't see what he was doing.

A fine white dust covered half an inch of the end of the screwdriver blade, enough to confirm Carlo's suspicions. He rubbed his finger on it, bent over just out of Ramirez's sight, and licked the dust off his fingertip. He'd only dabbled with these substances a little before being employed by Ernesto who, in no uncertain terms, had told him that in return for being paid handsomely, he would expect him not to become a user. It would affect his availability for work and he would be 'disposed of' if he was found incapacitated because of it. Carlo had taken him seriously. However, in the course of his work, he had taken the opportunity to be able to detect various substances and there was no doubt in his mind that this was what they were looking for.

Carlo gave himself a moment to think about what to do next. He put the pipes back down neatly where he had found them and continued to examine the contents of the pallet. There were several more packs of similar pipes that could potentially add up to the value of the shipment they were looking for. To avoid suspicion he tore open the shrink-wrap around each one and made it look like he'd checked them although he felt he didn't really need to. He thought that if he told Ramirez now the search would be over and he and Mary might renege on their deal to help look for Ricardo and disappear. He needed to keep looking busy for now while he worked out a plan, so he tidied up the shrink-wrap over the whole of the pallet of pipes and boxes and moved on to the next, a large crate that needed the wooden board removing from the top before he could see inside.

Ramirez's phone rang and he stood up and looked at the screen, "Problem in the sewage treatment plant. Back in a few minutes." Without looking at Carlo or waiting for him to speak, he left the room. Carlo took a breather and looked around the store room. A plan began to form in his mind. He reached for the first set of pipes he'd opened and stuck his little finger in the end he'd opened with the screwdriver, opening up the hole in the plastic. Then he tipped the pipes the other way and watched a puff of white powder escape onto the black shrink wrap. He squatted down next to the pallet and took out of his trouser pocket Ernesto's mobile phone, unlocked it with the code Ernesto had trusted him with, checked the background, and took a photo of himself, his white dust-covered finger and the small but obvious spray of powder on the black plastic-covered pallet.

Thinking for a moment and preparing himself for Ramirez to march back in at any second, Carlo opened up the messaging app and typed *I've found it*. When he'd finished he attached the photo and sent it.

To Ricardo.

Chapter 51

Ramirez had been back in the room for about ten minutes when a phone pinged again. This time it was Ernesto's phone, in Carlo's pocket. Carlo had expected a reply sooner but Ricardo must've taken his time thinking about it. That was a good sign. He opened up the message.

Found what?

Carlo excused himself to Ramirez and explained where his search was up to. Hopefully, Ramirez wouldn't double-check any of the places Carlo had already done, especially the one with the pipes. He said he'd be back in a few minutes, then walked out through the door and slowly down the corridor to a quiet corner by a staircase.

Your shipment, Carlo replied to Ricardo.

A minute later Ricardo sent, *Nothing to do with me.*

But who's going to believe that? Carlo was feeling more confident now that he had Ricardo where he wanted him. On the ropes. *You're not anonymous Ricardo. When they find this, and you, on this ship tomorrow morning, there's only one conclusion they'll come to. You are going away for a very long time. And your new empire will crumble before you've had time to establish it.*

A good five minutes passed before Ricardo replied. Carlo could imagine how angry this would make him and what names he'd be calling him right now. That was Carlo's plan. Ricardo had been naive in letting his personal feelings put him in a situation that he couldn't control. One that Ernesto had known was happening and would never have put himself into personally.

What do you want? Was the eventual and disappointingly obvious reply.

Carlo wondered if he really could expect Ricardo to pay him off, to say nothing about what he'd found, and not set him up tomorrow with the port authorities. He realised that a cleverer man than he could possibly work out how to get a pay-off from both Ricardo *and* Ramirez, pitting the two of them together while sneaking away from the situation. If he wasn't on a ship it might be possible, but he was realistic enough to understand that such scheming wasn't one of his strengths, and if he wanted to walk away from this business tomorrow there was no point doing it with dirty money in his pocket.

Chapter 52

Barker's phone buzzed in his trouser pocket. It was the first time that had happened for days. Nobody ever contacted him. He wondered who could possibly even have his number, other than Lucy who was standing next to him looking at Mary Tkachuk to see what her next move might be. He pulled the phone out of his pocket and turned slightly away from the group out of polite habit. He unlocked the screen and tapped the message that had just arrived, from a number he didn't recognise.

The message consisted of just an image. An image Carlo had obviously taken of himself in a crew store room somewhere. So he was OK. Barker felt a rush of relief. Carlo was crouched over a pallet with various shapes and sizes of packages wrapped together that he had clearly just opened up. He seemed to be pointing at a white patch on the black wrapping. Barker zoomed in with his fingers to see more clearly. The white patch was powder. It was on his finger and he was smiling at the camera. If that was what Barker thought it was, what was Carlo doing and why had he sent this image to them? Barker looked at the header information and saw that his was one of three numbers the image had been sent to. He didn't recognise any of the other numbers.

"What is it?" said Lucy, "What's wrong?"

Barker turned the phone around to show the image to Lucy and Stephen and didn't say anything, waiting to see their reactions. He carefully angled it so that Mary Tkachuk couldn't see it. Lucy's mouth just fell open before she said, "Carlo!" Stephen's face was expressionless but Barker detected something stirring behind his eyes.

"Why has he sent that?" said Lucy.

"Where is he?" said Stephen.

The three of them looked more closely at the image to scan for clues, keeping Mary out of the loop. Mary tried to look but didn't want to seem too desperate to find out. She'd not told them she'd seen Carlo, so why should she be interested? Yet she knew what he'd been doing the last time she saw him and couldn't help but wonder if he'd found what they'd been looking for.

Lucy grabbed the phone and zoomed the image out again, scanning it for clues to its location. Then she zoomed in on a sign on the wall in the background that said ENG001. "That's in engineering," she looked sideways at Mary as she said it and noticed her eyes light up with concern, "And if it's a pallet it must be in stores."

Barker took the phone from Lucy and examined the image for himself, "If we can work that out that quickly then someone else could too." Turning to Mary and noticing the discomfort in her eyes he wondered if this had anything to do with her. "Do you recognise these other phone numbers he's sent it to?" Mary leaned in and shook her head after a quick glance at the numbers and a scan of the small image. She was trying desperately to conceal her raised heart rate and flushing face. Where was Ramirez? Had Carlo done something with him? He was more than capable, despite what Ramirez would like to believe. Barker didn't know whether to believe her. "It could be he's sent it to Ricardo."

"Why would he do that?" said Lucy.

"I don't know, but who else could there be that he would want to know?"

"He can only have sent it because he wants us to go there," said Stephen, sounding more like an instruction than a suggestion.

Mary closed her eyes, took a deep breath and swallowed, before adding, "Drugs. It's a drug shipment."

"We can see that," said Lucy, thinking Mary was stating the obvious.

"It's *our* shipment," said Mary, releasing all the tension she'd been holding in, "Me and Jose are delivering it tomorrow in Florida. We paid to have it loaded today and hadn't located it. Jose was with Carlo looking for it. He wouldn't have agreed to this...whatever this is." Mary rattled the words out as if it was therapeutic to share the secret with someone. She knew this could mean the end of their plans but maybe that had happened already if Carlo had done something to Ramirez.

The three others stared at Mary for a few seconds absorbing this new information.

"What's this got to do with Ricardo?" said Stephen.

"Blackmail...maybe," said Barker, "And a really good way to lure Ricardo out."

"But it's nothing to do with Ricardo...is it?" Lucy said, turning to Mary, who shook her head.

"No," said Barker, "But who would believe that? A known cartel boss's son found on a cruise ship with millions of dollars worth of drugs. We know it's a coincidence but the border guards in the US won't buy that. Ricardo will be hunted down as soon as we dock tomorrow if anyone outside of us finds this out. He's got to get to Carlo before he tells anyone else."

"It looks like he's already told someone. Those other phone numbers..."

"None is them is Jose's," Mary added.

"Barker, Ricardo, and one other," said Stephen looking at the others for ideas, "Could he have told the authorities?"

"I don't think so. That would connect him to the shipment in their eyes. He would be foolish to do that unless there's more at stake. I think this is for people on this ship. I think he needs backup."

"We need to go there quickly before Ricardo gets to him," said Lucy.

"I can get us there fast," said Mary, "I know the shortest way and I know the codes for restricted areas."

Chapter 53

When Carlo's message with the image arrived Ricardo was at the aft of the ship outside the Skyscape restaurant on the same deck as the Lido, sitting at a table not far from the railings overlooking the ship's wake as it pushed powerfully through the sea towards Florida into the night. He'd positioned himself at an angle behind a family at a table next to him and with his back to a wall so that he could see people arriving in the area and turn away anonymously if he needed to. He'd dressed down in a T-shirt and jeans and wore a plain baseball cap. In the rucksack at his feet were the engineer's overalls he'd worn when boarding from the Pilot boat.

The messages from Carlo had wound him up as Carlo had no doubt intended. It was all Ricardo could do to restrain himself from shouting the obscenities that were in his head out loud. He'd shuffled at his table in temper while replying but when he calmed down he'd looked closer at the image and knew where he needed to be.

The engineering store room was twelve decks below where he was. All he had to do was get in a lift and go down but the normal lifts wouldn't take him all the way there. He walked into the nearby toilets and pulled on the overalls over his clothes, before heading out again and hanging around a crew-only lift.

After a couple of minutes, the lift doors opened and a chef from the kitchens stepped out, looking him up and down briefly whilst stepping out in a hurry and immediately disregarding him. Ricardo stepped into the lift and pressed the button for Deck Four where the engineering department was.

As the lift descended Ricardo felt uneasy. This was too easy. Carlo had worked for his father for a number of years and surely wasn't stupid enough to give away his location like that. Maybe he'd been over-excited to find a way of getting to him and forgotten himself and not checked his surroundings. Carlo wasn't much more familiar with this ship than he was so it could be a genuine mistake on his part, but he couldn't take the risk of walking into a trap that easily. So when the lift doors opened on Deck Four he didn't turn left and back on himself towards the stores, but walked straight out and across to the railings overlooking the back of the ship. There was a handful of other workers in various uniforms walking past in all directions and Ricardo realised he couldn't just hang around and watch. Thanks to the overalls he was wearing he would have to look busy to avoid suspicion.

Over to the port side of the railings was an open metal staircase with an electrical panel bolted to it. He had no idea what it was for but managed to hide himself behind it and hang his empty rucksack over the corner of it to make it look like he'd been sent to fix something. As long as nobody else was sent to mess with it or hung around in that spot for long enough to ask questions, he would be OK.

Chapter 54

With a renewed sense of purpose, Mary Tkachuk led Barker, Lucy and Stephen down a corridor out of the Atrium towards the aft of the ship. She was less worried about Carlo than she was about Ramirez. Carlo could look after himself, but what had happened to Jose? Maybe he knew what was going on and just didn't want to be in that photograph. Why would he? They were hours from a new life in the US. No need to ruin that now. And Ricardo didn't need to know about that.

Surprisingly, given that they had been on opposite sides most of the time, the others followed Mary unquestioningly, aware that she knew the ship better than any of them. Barker also knew that Lucy would have an idea where Mary was taking them so relied on her raising a red flag if she was unhappy about anything, but he kept that to himself.

They walked by a few passengers on the quiet section of cabins on Deck Five, most of whom were heading out to dinner. Then they got stuck behind a man pushing his wife in a wheelchair in the same direction they were heading. There wasn't enough room for them to pass but the man heard the group behind him and stopped next to a recessed cabin doorway and smiled as he let them walk by. It wasn't far until they arrived at the aft staircase and went down one floor to Deck Four. Barker had his Sea Star that would allow him pretty much anywhere on the ship, as did Mary, but Stephen was just a guest and felt a little out of place as Mary opened the crew-only door to the engineering section. Even Lucy had never been down here before.

There was a different kind of hustle and bustle going on here, with lots of people walking back and forth, up, down, and across the corridor, in and out of doorways. This was the beating heart of the ship where all the people who made the ship work went about their day, and it was staffed twenty-four-seven. Different kinds of machinery were spread out the full length of the ship over several decks: engines, water treatment, fuel storage, heating and cooling. But this was where the people responsible for it congregated to plan and work out how to keep everything running seamlessly.

"Just keep walking," said Mary, conscious that she had Stephen and Lucy following her, dressed like a couple of lost passengers. Fortunately, most of the regular employees knew her face and her reputation, and would not question why she had brought them down with her. They would know she had a reason and not care what that was, especially right now. The only exception would be the officers. She had to hope she didn't bump into any of them.

Stephen was unfazed but aware that he stuck out like a sore thumb so scanned around him carefully without making eye contact with any employees, instead purposefully following Mary like this was a normal occurrence. Lucy was a fish out of water. Despite being an employee there was no way any of the entertainment team would ever come down here. She counted on the fact that most of these guys spent their working lives here and may not have seen much of her before. They even had their own canteen where they could go in their overalls and not worry too much about mucking the place up.

Conscious that Mary might not have the same priorities as everyone else, Barker skipped past Lucy and Stephen and put his hand on her shoulder to ask her to stop. She almost jumped out of her skin.

"We need to be careful," whispered Barker as the four of them came to a halt a short distance from the aft of the ship on the starboard side. "Ricardo could be inside with Carlo already. Let me message him." Barker grabbed his phone to send a message to Carlo asking if it was safe to come and find him, but it wouldn't send. The ship's WiFi let him down. "Wait here. I'll go myself and come back and find you."

"I'm coming with you," Stephen said in a tone that made it sound like it wasn't up for debate.

"I was hoping you'd stay here with Lucy and Mary."

Stephen shook his head and gently pushed Barker forward towards the corner where they would turn to find the store room where Carlo should be. Barker accepted that maybe Stephen would be useful and slowly approached the corner of the corridor, peering round carefully and jumping back briefly when two men in overalls approached. He turned to face Stephen and held his phone up as if he was sharing some information with him, and the two engineers walked past with just a curious glance and a nod.

Barker felt a heavy hand on his shoulder as Stephen walked around him and said, "Wait here," and proceeded to walk towards the store room doors. Barker wasn't ready to let him approach the room on his own so followed him to the door.

Stephen looked annoyed with Barker, "I can do this myself. I don't need help."

OUT OF THE EQUATION

"You shouldn't go in on your own."

"So you open the door for me from that side and I'll stand here." Stephen shifted position right in front of where the door would open. "Ricardo doesn't know me. If he's in there and the door opens and he sees me he won't react the same as if he sees you or Lucy."

"What if he's armed?"

"I've had a gun pointed at me before John. He has no reason to shoot a stranger. Where would that get him?"

"OK," Barker said, "Enough messing around. Are you ready?" Stephen nodded and looked at the door. Barker gripped the stainless steel handle and pushed it down at the same time as pulling the heavy metal door outwards on its hinges. The light from the brightly lit store room reflected off Stephen as he stood looking inside. Barker could see his face from behind the open door. He took the lack of a sudden change in expression to be a good sign.

Stephen started to slowly walk into the store room and disappeared from Barker's view, who waited silently for a report. There was no noise from inside the room for five seconds or so until Stephen's voice said, "Carlo's here". Barker let out his held breath, sucked in more fresh air, and walked around to follow Stephen inside. He was about to say something to Carlo when there was a loud metallic thud behind him. All three jumped at the noise and turned to look at the door.

"The lock didn't turn," said Barker, wishing straight away that he hadn't, holding his breath a few more seconds in expectation of it doing just that.

"So?"

"A staff member would've either locked it or looked inside to see why it was open. Whoever slammed it didn't really care we were in here or already knew."

"Is there another way out?" said Stephen, looking around the room quickly for options and not finding any.

"He can't expect to come in here and take all three of us can he?" said Carlo.

"He might just wait it out," said Stephen, as the door clicked open gently.

The three of them turned to face the door again as a bent-over body stumbled through the gap and collapsed on the floor. It was Mary. Carlo stepped over to pick her up as the door closed behind her again. As he lifted her to her feet she looked up and Carlo saw blood coming from her nose and forehead. Somebody had smashed her face against a wall. Mary could barely stand and found it difficult to focus. She searched the room a couple of times before she locked on to Barker and tried to brace herself.

"He's got Lucy," Mary said.

The words hit Barker right in the stomach. Of course he's got Lucy. Everyone else is in here and he'd left her outside. How could he have been so stupid? Instead of luring Ricardo into a trap, they'd been lured into his. "Where?" Barker managed.

"Outside. He wants to talk."

"About what?" said Carlo.

"A deal," Mary wobbled as she spoke and turned as the door clicked open again behind her.

This time two people slipped sideways through the gap. In front was Lucy, stiffly shuffling with Ricardo behind her with his right hand over her mouth and his left hand jabbing a gun into her side. Lucy looked terrified. Barker felt sick. He stepped back as Ricardo and Lucy stood in the entrance, the door slightly ajar.

"Let her go," Barker said dutifully, despite how futile he knew

161

it was.

"She's my lifeline," growled Ricardo, "In more ways than one."

"You like hurting women?" Carlo added.

"I like using them to make men do what I want."

"So what *do* you want?" Barker said.

"I came here to kill you one by one to avenge my father. But I realise I'm outnumbered and you are cleverer than I expected you to be. So I will take the next best thing...money."

"Money?" said Carlo, "We have no money."

"No, but you have that," said Ricardo, pointing the gun momentarily at the pallet full of powder-filled pipes that Carlo had sent him an image of. "That will do nicely, thank you, Carlo. Lucy and I are going to leave now and find a nice cosy cabin somewhere to spend the night together. We can take our pick. The ship isn't full so most of them are empty and have been cleaned for the next guests. Nobody will disturb us." Lucy wriggled in disgust and Ricardo tightened his grip across her face and dug the gun in further. Barker made fists with his hands and gritted his teeth.

"You will all leave the ship in the morning as soon as the gangplank goes down," Ricardo continued, "And you will say nothing to anyone about what you found in here. I will let Lucy go when the shipment has been unloaded at another port of my choice. If anyone comes looking for me between now and then, poor Lucy will be found dead in the cabin, having suffered a horrible overdose. Does that sound fair?"

"No!" shouted Mary. "That's our future!" she cried out as she stumbled towards Lucy.

Stephen and Barker looked round in confusion at Mary's confession and grabbed her arms to stop her progress towards

Ricardo.

"I don't care about her," Mary said, trying to wave them away. Lucy's eyes widened in fear of the gun going off in her side as Ricardo shuffled them both back into the doorway.

"You no longer have a future Ms Tkachuk," said Ricardo, "Not with Ramirez anyway. I met him a few moments ago. He will not be joining us."

Just as Mary's knees were about to go from under her a sharp flash of metal appeared in the doorway into the right side of Ricardo's neck. A shower of blood squirted theatrically over the inside wall of the store room. Ricardo made no sound but briefly looked confused before the metal flashed out of his neck and his stomach arched forward, pushing into Lucy from behind. The hand over Lucy's mouth went limp and dropped to his side. His other hand did likewise allowing the gun to clatter to the floor. Ricardo's body crumpled slowly but inevitably down to the floor, bringing Lucy down on top of him.

Standing in the doorway with blood on her dress was Maria.

Chapter 55

"Surprise," Maria said deadpan, looking down at the body of Ricardo on the floor of the store room and watching the blood drip off the end of the knife she'd just pulled out of his back. Carlo spluttered at Maria in shock but had no time to ask how the hell she was still alive. Mary Tkachuk crawled on her knees towards the fallen gun but was beaten to it by Stephen, who grabbed it quickly and picked Lucy up by her shirt dragging her outside onto the aft deck towards the railings overlooking the ship's wake. A couple of stunned engineers passing by froze to the spot.

"What are you doing?!" said Lucy, in shock at finding the same gun being prodded into her side again by a different person.

"Taking over," said Stephen.

"Taking over what?" Barker asked.

"Everything," Stephen said calmly. "Firstly, Maria here, who we all thought was dead, seems to have opened up a vacancy in a successful local business. And I'm the first candidate to find out about it. Thank you, Maria. Secondly, that shipment over there is mine. I'm the buyer that Tkachuk and Ramirez were supposed to deliver it to tomorrow." Mary, still on the floor, looked up in horror. "But first I need Lucy."

Barker bristled and Lucy's heart missed a beat. "Me? What for?"

"It's understandable Lucy, that in all this you haven't realised one big thing. Something that I need you to give to me?"

"What do I have that you need?"

"Galaxy Cruise Line."

"What?"

"Ricardo isn't the only one that inherited a business today. Your father Aidan was the major shareholder in Galaxy if you remember. Didn't it occur to you that when you found him in the back of that SUV, that his stake had passed to you?"

Lucy was dumbstruck. It hadn't occurred to her at all and no words came out of her mouth, just noises.

"I see," said Stephen, "I thought not. I did some homework. You're an only child and your mother died almost ten years ago. So unless your father was a charitable man – and I knew him well enough to doubt that – then he will have left it all to you, by default rather than planning. So you have a choice."

"What choice?"

"There are two ways for you to pass your stake to me. One is to sign it over – I'll pay you a dollar. The other is for me to throw you over that railing outside and for you to disappear. When they eventually find your body I'll fight the other directors for control of that part of your estate. They're weak and will succumb eventually. They have no desire to increase their stakes or run a business that size. So it's up to you."

"I thought you came here for your family," interrupted Barker. "What about them?"

"This *is* for my family. I can set them up for life. My grandson will never have to worry about money."

"Just his granddad going to prison for supplying drugs," said

Lucy.

Barker's attention was on Stephen, dumbfounded at the latest development, wondering what his next move could be to stop him from hurting Lucy. Out of the corner of his eye, he saw movement about ten feet to Stephen's right behind some inflatable life rafts. Someone was approaching quietly and he seemed to recognise something about the shape of the movement. Then it dawned on him when he saw the face. Ashton. What on earth...? Barker's heart raced but he fought the urge to react. What was he doing here? Whose side was he on this time? Fortunately, the decision became clear as events unfolded in front of him.

"So what's it to be Lucy?" said Stephen as he raised the pistol pointed at her head. Ashton saw Stephen's arm raise and shouted, "Put it down."

Stephen, surprised, turned his head, giving Barker the cue to make his decision. He could have gone to grab Lucy and pull her out of the way, but he was just too far away to do it cleanly, and with a gun being waved around there was a chance she would get hurt.

The decision he made was the most impulsive of his life and he knew it would save Lucy. But as he bent his knees and launched himself into a sprint towards Stephen he knew he hadn't considered the consequences for himself. It didn't matter.

Stephen spun around to his right and brought his arm around with the pistol, but Ashton was never going to let him get away with that, firing a shot into his shoulder that knocked him off balance but didn't take him down. Stephen recovered enough to lift the gun again and Barker couldn't take the risk that Ashton could stop him before he fired at Lucy.

"John!" Lucy shouted.

Barker's momentum carried his eighty-kilo weight at full speed right into the centre of Stephen's body and smacked him backwards into the railings with a sickening snapping sound of bone against metal. But it didn't stop there. Barker had gone too high and grabbed Stephen around the shoulders as his weight bowled him back, up and over the railings.

Lucy's lasting memory would be of the two men lifting up in the air in slow motion, inverting over the railing, and dropping down into the sickening black void below. It was one of those times when you simply can't believe what you've seen and you want to rewind time and pause it before it could happen. She screamed the deepest scream from her gut and shouted into the wake of the ship. "Nooo!"

Chapter 56

Lucy had collapsed face first, fully clothed onto the bed in the hotel room in Port Everglades in Fort Lauderdale shortly after midnight, after Starlight had turned around and searched for Barker in the dark Atlantic ocean for nearly two hours before leaving the search to the coastguard and heading for port. Her eyes were red raw from tears and the energy that had kept her going through the longest day of her life, during which she'd lost her father and her partner, finally ran out and she fell into immediate unconsciousness.

She dreamt of the torment of watching Barker disappear into the black again and again, dwarfing all the horrors they'd witnessed in the previous three weeks. She dreamt of throwing a lifebuoy into the sea and remembered the staff that had streamed out to help and raise the alarm. She dreamt of the sound of the 'man overboard' alarm on Starlight and the interminable wait for the coastguard boats to arrive while Starlight circled and she squinted into the darkness for any signs of life. She dreamt of being carried hysterically off the ship into a car and being driven the short distance to the hotel by persons unknown. She hadn't cared. They'd left her standing in the doorway promising to 'keep her informed'. She'd thrown up in the sink and passed out on the bed.

"Lucy?"

"Lucy? It's me.....afmdnjk."

Lucy thought she was still dreaming but now there was a thudding noise. Probably her head, or her heart. She didn't move as she drifted in and out of consciousness.

"It's me. Ashton."

Why do I know that name? Another thud, louder this time.

Somebody's banging on the door, she thought, "Go away!" she tried to say but only "Gmnfmmfh" came out of her mouth into the bed covers.

The next thing she knew she was being lifted off the bed into a chair. She waved her arms around to stop whoever it was from touching her. She tried to focus on the face of the man in front of her. There were two of them. One in uniform holding a piece of plastic, a door key. He must've let them in. The other man she recognised. Friendly, half-smiling.

Asmam. Asdon. Ash...Ashton. What's he doing here? What did he want now? She flinched as she remembered him, unsure whether to trust him.

"They've found him, Lucy. He's alive. He's in a bad way but he's alive. He's in the hospital. We can go now."

Chapter 57

One Week Later

"Boring isn't it?" said Lucy with a smile as she walked into the private room in the hospital where Barker was recovering. She had visited him every day since he'd been rescued from the sea off the coast of Miami, hypothermic and with lungs half full of seawater, but he'd been in a coma for the first few days and then only barely able to recognise her when she spoke to him.

"What is?" Barker replied, shuffling to sit up in his hospital bed as Lucy sat down in a plastic chair next to him. Today was the first time he felt strong enough to actually have a proper conversation with her. His memory of the last moments on Starlight was very patchy and he needed to catch up.

"Sitting in a hotel bed for a week waiting for something to happen, or to be told you can go home."

"I don't think I'm ready to go anywhere just yet, and I'll take boredom over anything else right now. We've had enough drama for a lifetime."

"Oh I hope not. I was beginning to enjoy it," Lucy said with a smile.

"Liar."

"Well look at what we've done. We've cruised across oceans,

solved murders, met some great people and some terrible people. We've disposed of one or two who won't be missed…" Lucy's voice trailed off as she looked around the room to make sure no-one else had heard her say that. The door was closed and she couldn't see anyone through the window panel onto the corridor.

"And we've lost a bit too," said Barker, thinking of his ex-wife Laura and Lucy's father Aidan, "Lucy, about your dad…he was…"

"In the fire. I know that John."

"When?"

"When we drove away and I heard the explosion. That's when it occurred to me you wouldn't have left him in the boot."

"I'm sorry."

"It's OK. His choice. Live by the sword, die by the sword, and all that. But we've come through it and it's a brighter day. Or it will be when we get you out of here. We're in Florida!"

"What about Stephen? Have you heard any news about him?"

"How many times are you going to ask me that question? That's all I managed to get out of you for the last couple of days, in your semi-comatose state. You seemed more bothered about him than me."

"Sorry, you know that's not the case. But I worry he'll turn up somewhere unless they find his body. I think it'll take a long time to shake that feeling."

"No bodies have been found along that stretch of coastline in the past week. The police are sick of me asking, so I talked to the coastguard myself. You were found by a group of college friends out fishing. They were almost too drunk to lift you out of the water but one of them managed it. They said nothing about seeing another body. Besides, you hit him pretty hard into the railings. I think he was dead when he hit the water."

"Did you find out what Ashton was doing on the ship?"

"Yes. He felt so bad after he met you at the gates that day that he sent his wife and daughter home in the taxi, got his gun and ID from the port office, and got back onto the ship, through the cargo entrance just before it closed. Understandably he thought we might not welcome him back so he kept an eye on us from a distance. Of course, he'd heard about what had happened to Ernesto and guessed that Ricardo would come looking for us so had to keep himself hidden in case Ricardo recognised him."

"How did he manage to turn up when he did?"

"Apparently his police department got an anonymous tip-off from someone on board Starlight, to say they'd seen Ricardo on board and even gave them the location of the shipment. The only other people who could've known that were the people who'd arranged to have it loaded – the couple that Mary Tkachuk paid with the diamonds."

"Ah, Mary. How is she?"

"Back at work on Starlight with a completely different outlook on life. I think losing Ramirez has affected her a lot. She's much calmer and quieter and, believe it or not, friendlier. So I'm told by some of the people I've kept in touch with."

"She didn't get into any trouble?"

"No, she's in the clear. There was no evidence linking her or Ramirez to the shipment other than the couple who took the diamonds, and they vanished. The police believe it was all down to Ricardo...and Carlo."

"Carlo?"

"Yes, he'd put his prints all over it, hadn't he? I think he knew the trouble he was in because he just disappeared, along with some of the spare parts the drugs were hidden in."

Barker shook his head slowly, amazed at how it had all unravelled.

"Talking of people who've disappeared..." said Lucy.

"Mmm?" Barker did his best to not know what was coming next.

"You know very well who I mean."

"No idea."

"Maria hasn't been seen since that moment in the doorway, thanks to Stephen distracting everybody's attention. She must've taken the opportunity to disappear."

"How did she get off the ship?"

"Officially she didn't. They delayed Starlight leaving Miami as long as possible before the next cruise had to set off. She must've found a way off without being scanned."

Barker just nodded gently in agreement.

"Which brings me to a few questions."

"Do you have to? I'm quite tired."

"In your delirium when they found you, you mumbled something to me about her not really being dead and asked where she was."

"Did I? I don't remember that."

"You did. And I don't believe you," said Lucy trying to hide the smile growing on her face. "I wondered how she could fake her own death when you'd tried to resuscitate her for ten minutes. Unless of course you were in on it and weren't actually trying all that hard."

Barker shrugged and did his best to look innocent, as if he had no idea what Lucy was talking about.

"You cooked it up between you didn't you?"

"It seemed like a good idea at the time?"

"I bet it did."

"We needed a backup option. If she disappeared and Ricardo found out about it he would discount her and she could hide away until the time was right. It was a gamble but it worked."

"How did she know where to be, and when?"

"That other number that Carlo sent the photo to...of him in the store room? It was Maria's. She put two and two together and turned up in the right place. As for timing, I don't know, maybe that was just good luck."

"So Carlo knew as well?"

"Yes."

"Why couldn't you have faked my death instead? I could've done with a break."

"Ricardo didn't care enough about you."

"Thanks. None taken. So basically you kissed a semi-naked Maria and massaged her chest for ten minutes?"

"A little bit."

"In front of me."

"Guilty."

"Unbelievable."

"What about the cruise line?" said Barker desperately trying to change the subject.

"I sold my shares. Turns out Stephen was wrong. The other directors were all keen to take up my offer, to keep the company in safe hands, they said. So I've had a windfall you could say. Not that you're going to see any of it after what you got up to."

"Talking of windfalls, whatever happened to the cash?"

"I was wondering when you were going to ask about that."

"I've been in a coma for four days...You said it was 'close'"

"Any excuse. Well yes, by close I meant on the ship."

"Starlight?"

"Duh. Where else? Carlo had a contact in the crew he rang

on the way to the port. They were doing a lifeboat drill as we arrived."

"I remember watching from the window."

"So we backed the SUV up onto the quayside and stuffed the bags under the seats in one of the half-dozen lifeboats they were using – not one of the tenders they would use to and from a port, so it stayed untouched."

"...And."

"And I told the band where it was...and Kendall who helped you with the chandelier...and asked them to share it amongst the crew. They should all get a few thousand dollars each if they've done it properly. Oh, and Ashton might find a new car on his driveway next week. I didn't think it was wise for him to have a share in stolen cash, being a policeman. But this way there shouldn't be too many questions."

"You've been busy."

"Stops me being bored."

About the Author

Steven Lea loves writing books but hates writing about himself, especially in the third person. He loves to travel with his wife, especially on cruises. No surprises there. He especially loves reviews left online by the wonderful human beings who read his books (thank you).

You can connect with me on:
- http://www.stevenlea.com
- https://www.facebook.com/stevenleaauthor
- https://www.instagram.com/stevenleaauthor

Subscribe to my newsletter:
- http://www.stevenlea.com

Also by Steven Lea

Other books in this series: Out of His Depth, Out of Their League

Please keep an eye on my website and social media for news of new releases and upcoming projects. Better still, sign up for my newsletter.

Thanks for reading.

Printed in Great Britain
by Amazon

29268178R00108